Amish Dawn

Amanda Reese

Published by Trellis Publishing, 2021.

AMISH DAWN

First edition. June 29, 2021.

Copyright © 2021 Amanda Reese.

ISBN: 979-8224689453

Written by Amanda Reese.

AMISH DAWN

AMANDA REESE

Chapter 1: Times Like This

Dawn Wittmer always thought of herself as a simple girl, and was a simple girl in the eyes of everyone, except her parents. Everything that Dawn did was wrong. How could it be that such a simple girl was never good at doing anything? Dawn knew that her parents were quite strict, but still, she wondered why she never earned their satisfaction. Her parents' disapproval came out in ways that she preferred not to consider, such as her poor self-esteem. Even when she was selling the family's produce in the market she found herself stressed and worried that she would do something wrong, give incorrect change, or lose customers by not providing the service and prices that the customers wanted.

Dawn knew so little about life; sometimes she wanted her world to be just at least a little bit bigger than the world that her parents imagined for her. Dawn would have loved to have permission to just be a little bit, well, "normal." Some of her other Amish friends had permission to go out of the house, have English friends, and even on a rare occasion have a beer or a glass of wine. She didn't want to leave the Amish community but recently the way her parents had been treating her like she was a 7-year-old again was making her go crazy and feel more anxious.

Dawn wasn't seven years old and she knew that very well. She was 18 years old and graduating school this year. She'd learned more from studying on her own than she gained from attending school in the one room schoolhouse that her parents insisted she attend. Dawn dreamed of attending university, of becoming a nurse, and helping those who were sick. She didn't agree with everything that the Amish believed, such as their views regarding medicine and the use of it. Why shouldn't those who are very sick utilize medicine if they have the chance to make use of modern medicine that could save their lives? Why did her parents have to see everything in "black and white?" Everything was always good or bad. In other words, everything was Amish or English and if it was English that meant it was not acceptable.

If her parents knew about her views on medicine or that sometimes she drank wine with her friends they would be so angry that she probably could not stay in their home. What was so terrible about having a glass of wine? She wanted to know. The smell of a nice glass of Merlot or Cabernet Sauvignon would make her evening. Just that little feeling that lifted her mood ever so slightly. She could feel the stress melt away from her heart, her head, her soul, her body with just one glass of wine. Sometime when she visited her friend Beth Troyer they would sit and play Scrabble together, passing the time, laughing, and talking. What neither her parents nor Beth's parents knew was that an English friend of Beth's would buy her wine. Sometimes she paid her friend with money if she had any, and other times with baked goods.

Beth understood Dawn. They had been friends since they were little and even though neither one wanted to consider leaving the Amish community they had some complaints with the rules. Why were there so many rules?

Chapter 2: Market Days

Dawn's life continued. Her days at the market were long. Secret Scrabble and wine nights were few and far between. Plus, it was hard for Beth to sneak the wine into her room and get it cold. There was almost no way to get the wine cold unless her English friend brought the wine already chilled and they consume it immediately.

Among the rows of sellers in the market were both English and Amish vendors. The cost of renting the space was increasing yet their sales remained more or less the same. The same customers. The weeks melted into each other, seeming almost entirely the same. She hardly had any schoolwork to do and she knew that her parents would never let her attend college. What was the point? Recently one of the other storefront owners was coming around to her store almost every day. It was almost annoying. Actually, it was annoying. Sunny Landsdale was his name. He was a fairly tall young man with wide shoulders, and his hair was pulled back in a ponytail, as if he wanted to be a girl. His name sounded much like a name for a girl too. She thought he was a little strange, but perhaps some part of him could be likeable. Dawn's thoughts drifted to her Amish upbringing. God asks us to love everyone, not just the people we like or love. Certainly, it was her job to treat everyone with respect that came to her stand, whether or not she liked her family's customers. She convinced herself to make small talk with Sunny. She even wanted to get up the nerve to ask him why he didn't cut his hair. Maybe today would be the day she would ask him.

Among the other fruit and pastry sellers, Dawn sat at her stand amid crates of tomatoes, cucumbers, onions, garlic, corn, and even carrots when Sunny approached the stand again. Perhaps more annoying than his hair was the fact that he stopped by more or less just to chat. He didn't seem to have any objective except bothering her! Was this the goal? This could hardly be the goal. Of course, it also seemed strange that he would come and buy just a single tomato or onion. He claimed that he bought fresh ingredients every day to cook dinner. Dawn presumed that although this could be true, he also apparently came around to her stand just to speak to her. Although many other people would consider this a compliment she preferred to do her work and be left alone. Not to mention that she had heard some interesting things about him. Some stories that she hoped were not true. She heard he had multiple lovers, all customers. She didn't want to hear anymore.

"My dearest Dawn, you are looking beautiful as always. Although I bet you would look stunning in a long, sleek, black evening gown! You are quite a beauty. What can I say?" said Sunny. "Well, you could say less. That would be a great start," replied Dawn. "Oh, my lovely, one day you will be my wife, just you see! But, in the meantime I will have to wait for you to choose to leave your Amish community and run away with me. Of course, a man cannot wait forever!" declared Sunny with enthusiasm. Dawn rolled her eyes and asked him, "So, what can

I get for you today, Mr. Landsdale: a single tom..." Sunny interrupted her midsentence. "I thought we discussed that my name is Sunny. Still you prefer to refer to me as Mr. Landsdale. Mr. Landsdale is my father, thank you very much."

"As you wish, Sunny," Dawn heard herself say. She couldn't help but thinking about how silly his name and hair were. Sunny laughed and Dawn paused before posing her question. "Mr. Landsdale, ahem, I mean, Sunny, did you ever realize that, between your hair and your name, some people may think some strange things about you. I don't mean to be rude, but you can hear all kinds of gossip about a boy with a name like Sunny!" Dawn offered this observation with some courage. Sunny simply laughed, "Actually, I love my name, and yes, my hair too. You wanted to ask about my hair, I'm sure. No?" asked Sunny. "Well, yes, I hadn't quite gotten there yet," said Dawn.

"Well, to tell you the truth, since you know, I'm always honest about everything, like your good looks for example... anyway, as I was saying. My Dad always cut my hair very short when I was a kid and I hated it. When I finally got old enough to make my own decisions about my hair, I decided to stop cutting it. My whole family went crazy, but then they got used to it, and I realized I actually quite liked it. So, I kept it. Now the hair goes better with my name too! It keeps people on their toes," answered Sunny.

"You certainly are at least an interesting person," answered Dawn. Sunny smiled as a slightly extended pause in the conversation ensued. "Right, anyway, I need three green peppers for dinner tonight," said Sunny. "Sure, wow. Three, not one?" joked Dawn. "Yes, three," echoed Sunny as a goofy grin spread across his face. Sunny handed over $1.00, took his green peppers and walked away back toward his stand.

Dawn found herself watching him as he walked away and couldn't understand what or why she was watching. He was such a strange man. Dawn shook her head and continued scouring the market, hoping to make eye contact with potential customers. Business had been slower than usual this summer with no thanks to the opening of a super Wal-Mart on the south side of the city. That's what she guessed anyway. It's difficult to maintain customers and gain new ones when giant corporations can roll into town and capitalize on the local people's inability to lower prices to an unreasonable point. As Dawn grew lost in her thoughts about the super Wal-Mart and even surprisingly about herself the market day grew to a close. She carefully put away all the unsold food, locked the cabinets, and made her way home by foot.

Chapter 3: A Patient Man

Jane and Mason Wittmer, Dawn's parents, did not see positive changes in Dawn. In fact, they were ready to sit down with their daughter and discuss with her their knowledge of this Sunny boy. Jane and Mason were respected by the entire Amish community and were well-known and respected even in the marketplace. It had come to their attention that Sunny Landsdale, a known associate of the Amish Mafia was purchasing goods from their store, which in and of itself, is not a crime. They did not appreciate, however, that he was making conversation with their daughter. Parents know best, of course. Anyone even vaguely connected with Amish Mafia was not a friend of theirs. They didn't like what they know about Sunny. They even considered removing Dawn from the market stand to keep Sunny away from her.

Jane and Mason decided that they needed to sit down with their daughter and discuss this situation that was ever so pressing on their minds. A good Amish daughter did her work, stayed away from unnecessary conversation with any English man, worked on the farm or in the market, prayed, and did her homework. Dawn could be quickly headed down the wrong path. On the evening following the day of the three green peppers, Jane and Mason decided to summon their daughter to the sitting area.

"Dawn!" Jane called up the stairs. "We need you to come downstairs for a minute." Dawn immediately knew that those words meant "we want to have a serious conversation with you." A million and one things were passing through Dawn's mind. Did they found out that she and Beth had been sneaking wine into the community and drinking sometimes? Will they forbid her to apply to college?

"Dawn. We want you to stay away from the Sunny boy," said Jane. "Any questions?" asked Mason, Dawn's father. Dawn stayed silent. "No comment at all?" inquired her mother. "Well, yes: you know it's not my fault who comes to buy food at our store. What, you want me to put out a sign that says only GOOD people buy food here! Are you crazy?" said Dawn. "Enough!" shouted Mason. "We just want you to be a little careful with Sunny. Don't make conversation. Give him what he purchases and be sure to count the change extra carefully. Okay?" said Jane.

"Sure, Mom... whatever," answered Dawn as she rolled her eyes without realizing what she was doing until it was too late. "Not whatever, do not talk to your Mom with that tone of voice, and don't let me see you roll your eyes again!" shouted Mason. "Yes, Dad. May I be excused?" "Yes, thank you Dawn," whispered Jane in a small voice.

As Dawn crept back up the winding wooden staircase to her room she considered the conversation. Although she was annoyed by the way they had accused her of engaging in conversation with Sunny, she was more relieved that they didn't know about the wine. She wasn't a drunk. She didn't need a drink. She just liked a glass of wine once in a while. That hardly made her a sinner, or evil, did it? She didn't think that made her a sinner. In the Bible, Mary asked Jesus to turn water into wine during a wedding when the couple ran out of wine to serve their guests. Dawn silently recounted the parable to herself and reminded herself that she was not a bad person. She simply had difficult, traditional Amish parents.

She continued working at the market after the confrontation with her parents. But as if he'd been warned away, Sunny was suddenly making himself scarce. She wondered where he had gone. Was he okay? She chided herself for thinking about whether or not he was okay. Why was she worried about Sunny? Sunny, his girlish name, his bleached pony tail, and cocky smile. What a silly man; no... what a silly boy. How old was he anyway? After a week of managing the store in the market and seeing no sign of Sunny, Dawn was just about ready to accept that he had found another girl to flirt with. Or, perhaps, he'd left town. Types like Sunny didn't usually stick around too long. But just then there was a tap on her shoulder. "Good afternoon, Ms. Wittmer. How are you today?" asked Sunny. "Just fine, thank you, but um... where have you been?" asked Dawn.

"Ah! So, you missed me, right? I knew it! I knew you'd miss me!" replied Sunny, a huge grin spreading across his face. "No, I didn't say that. I just said, where have you been?" retorted Dawn. "Of course, as you see it. Busy. That's all," replied Sunny. "Okay, so what can I get you today?" asked Dawn.

"Well, actually, I don't need any green peppers, but I did want to know if you'd like to accompany me for a smoothie!" invited Sunny in a bright, ironically sunny way. "You mean, um, like a date?" asked Dawn. "Yes. Or no. Whatever you would like it to be," replied Sunny. "You know, I'm not... um, I'll think about it," said Dawn. "You'll think about it. Okay: well, I can be a patient man. Let me know, let's say tomorrow, about our non-date. It's just a smoothie," Sunny pointed out diplomatically.

With that, Sunny turned and walked backed into the crowd of the market. Dawn found herself standing at the counter trying to catch her breath. Yes, for certain, Sunny had just asked her out on a date. Were her parents correct in saying to stay away from him? What if they were just wrong about him? It wouldn't be the first thing they were wrong about. She never had English friends before because her family forbid it. She was just curious enough what it would be like to go out with an English boy that she contemplated saying yes. As she closed the store for the day she found herself poised between her family's values and wanting to discover herself and the world for herself.

Chapter 4: More Than Just Coffee

The next day as Sunny approached the counter, without even thinking Dawn said, "Yes." Surprised, Sunny said, "Ok then, I'll be back at close to 4pm to meet you!" As Sunny turned to walk away, Dawn said, "Wait, make it 3pm outside the back entrance of the market." "Anything for my sunshine!" replied Sunny and laughed, since, after all, his name was sunshine, not hers. At precisely 3pm Dawn closed the store one hour earlier than usual and met him outside the market. Dawn found Sunny waiting for her there. "It's just a few blocks away," said Sunny.

As they walked Dawn realized she didn't know what to say at all. It was as if someone had glued her lips together. Sunny, recognizing the pause and potential awkwardness, started talking about himself. "Well, since you don't know a lot about me, I'll tell you the saga, if you want." "Sure," answered Dawn.

"I grew up in several different foster homes, bounced from one to another, and usually I ran away because my foster parents would beat or just use me for the government check. You know?" Sunny began his remarkable tale as if it were commonplace. "Actually, I'm sorry, I'm not understanding, because you know I'm Amish," admitted Dawn. Sunny started again, in an attempt to clarify: "When I was young, my parents died in a car accident. I was 4 years old. Just old enough to remember them and miss them. When you become an orphan, or your parents don't want you, the state tries to find a placement for you with another family in another home. But sometimes, these homes are dangerous. There aren't enough controls and regulations on who can become a foster parent." "Oh, I'm sorry. I had no idea," said Dawn. "Don't be. I'm just sharing with you my story. As soon as I turned 18 I was out of the system because I became a legal adult. I was homeless for a little while until I found a job at one of the stands here. They pay me cash under the table. No taxes or anything. Since then I've saved enough money to get a place, but I've never finished school. I want to get my GED someday, but that seems like a dream." said Sunny.

There was another pause in the conversation, but this time, perhaps it was a needed pause. "And now, how are you?" Dawn asked with genuine concern. "I'm well, just me," said Sunny. "But, why did you tell me this other story about your hair and your parents, when you don't have parents?" asked Dawn. "I wanted to impress you," Sunny confessed. "I didn't want you think I was just some orphan kid. In the beginning, I kept my hair long because my foster parents would rarely give me a haircut, let alone pay for me to get one. Sometimes they would destroy my hair when they cut it. So, finally, when I aged out of foster care, I decided nobody was going to cut my hair like that again, even me," explained Sunny.

"Well, anyway, that's me. How about those smoothies?" Sunny invited, apparently ready to change the subject. "Of course," said Dawn. As they sat together in the Tropical Smoothie Café, Dawn imagined that in some ways she had never considered before, she'd been given more opportunities in her strictly controlled life than an English man like Sunny. She wanted to tell him that her parents would freak out if they knew she had come out with him even for a smoothie, but then again, she thought it might be better if she said nothing. He probably could have guessed as much anyway. As they continued talking, Sunny moved his hand across the table and placed it on top of Dawn's hand. Dawn was startled and considered moving it. But she found that she didn't want to move it. Nobody in the Amish community would be this open with another. No one would tell someone else who wasn't in his or her family personal things. Why couldn't she trust Sunny? It was true he was two years older than she was, but two years was nothing. Plus, they were both legal adults, and hand-holding wasn't a crime.

Finally, Dawn got up the nerve to ask Sunny about the gossip at the market. "Sunny, can I ask you something?" Dawn inquired. "Sure," replied Sunny. "Is it true that you... you know... with other girls. Like am I just one of a bunch of other girls?" asked Dawn. "Oh, no... actually I just ignore the gossip at the market. One of my old foster parents owns a stall in the market so they made up stories about me to try to make me lose my job, but it didn't work," replied Sunny. "Oh, I thought... sorry," whispered Dawn. "Don't be, it's not a problem."

Just then Dawn looked at the clock on the wall and realized it was 4:20. If she didn't all but run home her parents would know something was up. Dawn jumped up and said a little louder than necessary, "Oh, I have to leave quickly... if I don't get home soon..." "It's a problem, right? Your parents I'm sure wouldn't like seeing someone like me with their daughter. Right?" interrupted Sunny. "Actually, yes I'm really sorry. Please. I have to go. I'll see you tomorrow at the market?" asked Dawn, "Yes, don't worry, just g,." replied Sunny.

Chapter 5: Learning to Fly

They knew. Before Dawn even made it inside the door, Jane and Mason were waiting for Dawn at the kitchen table. How could I be so stupid, thought Dawn. Of course, someone would have noticed that she closed the store an hour earlier. As Dawn approached her parents, her father started screaming, so loud, that even the neighbors on the opposite end of the community would hear him. She was positive. "Dawn. You're going to your uncle's! We're sending your disobedient soul away! You need to learn respect, and the importance of NOT LYING TO YOUR FAMILY! End of discussion! You will not go back to the marketplace tomorrow. You will not see Sunny Landsdale ever again! Do you hear me?" raged Dawn's father Mason.

Dawn stood in silence in the kitchen and held back tears. Mason continued screaming. "Do you know what filth people like Sunny are? He is nothing. Nobody. He is a cheater and he hangs around with the type of people we do NOT associate with! Do you understand me? We know for a fact that he has purchased a gun from the Amish Mafia. We don't know why he has a gun or wanted a gun, but you cannot speak to him ever again. ARE WE CLEAR?" bellowed Mason

Dawn could do nothing except nod her head yes. Then she ran to her room. She wanted to find Beth and tell her everything. She wanted even more to speak to Sunny. Her parents didn't understand him. They didn't know him. And if he owns a gun, Dawn was sure that there was a reason. Sunny was a good man. They didn't know anything. Who were her parents to tell her about Sunny anyway? Dawn was overcome with outrage. They knew nothing. How could it be that her parents never saw anything in another way? They saw only things the way they wanted to see them! Nothing else!

Tomorrow she would be sent away. The worst thing was that Sunny would once again have one less person to speak to. He was on his own. But what was worse? Having no family, or a family that doesn't understand you and let you be who you want to be? Family should be the center or everything, the center of life, the center of love. Without family we are alone—unless of course you believe in God. Even with God on your side, you can feel lost and alone. There is something unique about having a human companion. Dawn longed to have her own family and her own companion. For the last year or two, she had felt part of a family that, although she knew loved they her very much, she felt the need to be separated from them. Was it selfish, she wondered? Maybe it was just a part of growing up, she thought.

Dawn found herself lost in her own thoughts about life. As we grow up we see life in a different light, sometimes for better, and sometimes for worse. We learned to see things through our own lenses. We saw things the way we wanted to see them. Sometimes that was a better choice and sometimes not. We learned that life does not happen in black and white. Life is an ever-changing revolving door. As we grow up we learn that a whole world exists outside the bubble that our parents gave us. Then the only option we have is to make our decisions and choose whether or not we want to fly.

Chapter 6: Nowhere to Run or Hide

The events that followed the day of the smoothie were a blur to both Dawn and Sunny. Sunny went to Dawn's family's stand to find it closed. He was concerned but decided not to worry too much. For certain something had come up at home. Then again, that was also what he was worried about. What happened at home? Was it because he met her outside the market? Did someone see them together?

Sunny began panicking, but not too much, because like always, he found a solution. He knew how to handle almost every possible problem. Running he was good at. Actually, it was his specialty. So was hiding. The thing about being a former foster kid is that you learn how to run and hide. He didn't want to run this time. He finally had a job, an address, a roof over his head. Sunny passed the whole week trying not to be concerned when the stand didn't open. Finally, a week later the stand opened again, but still Dawn was nowhere to be found. A woman, probably Dawn's mother, was operating their fruit and vegetable stand. He knew that asking her where Dawn was could make things worse for Dawn so he simply passed the stand slowly looking for any sign that Dawn had been there or was okay.

As he passed the woman at the stand studied him with a fierce gaze. Her eyes followed Sunny across the market and watched his every move. Very conscious of the fact that he was being watched, he ducked out of the market and cut down an alley in the opposite direction of his apartment. If this was life, he wasn't sure why he existed. Perhaps worse than being orphaned was the knowledge that his mother had been pregnant when his parents died in the car crash. He never knew what it was like to have a sister or brother, but guessed that if he had been left with a brother or sister, at least they could have been there for each other.

Meanwhile Dawn woke up on the far side of the Pennsylvania border. The sun rose over Tennessee on her Uncle Kemp's property. Uncle Kemp was a quiet stern man with rules, a wood-burning stove, and a dog. Uncle Kemp never married and most of the family thought he was slightly strange. Dawn's uncle left the Amish years ago and was rarely in contact with his family. He left the community not because he minded the simple life, but actually, because he'd had a relationship with an English girl and was banished from the house. After the relationship ended, he didn't want to be with anyone else, quite literally. He took the failed union as a sign that he was to live alone.

Nobody even knew what he did to make a living and nobody asked either. Dawn found some small comfort in her Uncle's cooking and the dog, a Yorkshire Collie with thick white and black fur. She loved nothing more than to cuddle up to him, especially when she needed to cry, which was more often than not these days. She helped her Uncle Kemp in all but silence as she learned to cut wood for the fire, maintain the property, and prepare meals for the two of them.

Her parents must have thought that sending her away to her Uncle's would make her beg to come home. Dawn was not going to beg to come home. That was not part of her plan. She would stay here as long as they made her stay. She didn't care about anything. Well, almost anything. There was the issue of Sunny. She found herself thinking about where Sunny was or if Sunny thought she left the market to avoid him, or perhaps he thought that she didn't like him. Actually, the opposite was true. She was realizing that she did like him, more than she thought she did.

Chapter 7: Connections

The difficult part of finding a missing person is that either the person does not want to be found, or is being held against their will. There were few to no clues about the whereabouts of Dawn. Due to Sunny's long history of learning how to survive, hide, and get needed information, Sunny knew that if he was patient, eventually he would find out where Dawn had disappeared to. He lurked around the market listening for any information about her whereabouts. Most of the sellers at Amish community stands were tight lipped. If they knew something, they weren't telling. Many of the regulars didn't know anything about Dawn, but sellers at neighboring stands, with whom Dawn was friendly, surely did. About two weeks had passed before Sunny had a stroke of luck. He was standing in the line of shops behind the row where Dawn's family's store was located. He overhead a conversation that he had been waiting to hear.

"...too bad about Dawn, really. She is a nice girl," said the one candle shop owner.

"I always thought those Amish people were a bit strange," replied the lady who owned the pastry stand.

"You know, I heard they took her away entirely. To Tennessee, I think. Yeah, the mother said to me that she was going to her Uncle Kemp's place to stay awhile. Who knows how long she'll be gone," answered the candle shop owner.

"If I didn't know any better, I would have thought those two were together anyway. Maybe they were an item, you know," said the pastry stand owner.

"Anyway, it's better to keep your eyes to your own business," stated the candle shop owner.

That was all Sunny needed to hear. They took her out of state to Tennessee to an Uncle Kemp's house. Not as much information as he would have liked, but it was certainly a good start. It had been two weeks already since he last saw Dawn and he wasn't going to let the smoothie date be the last one.

Sunny informed his employer he was going on a personal business trip and hoped that he would still have his job and his apartment when he returned. He just paid the rent again so for now he would be okay.

Sunny left the next morning before dawn broke. He paused thinking about how lovely dawn was and how perfectly named his friend Dawn was. He would find her. With a one-way bus ticket to

Nashville, Tennessee, a granola bar, a water bottle, a change of clothes, an extra pair of boxers, a smartphone and charger, a half-full small notebook with a pen in the spiral binding, and a paper map of Tennessee in his backpack, Sunny boarded the Greyhound. Sunny knew Greyhound buses very well. More than once he'd had to utilize a fake ID to buy a Greyhound ticket to escape a foster family. Although Sunny mused it was probably unnecessary to find Dawn as she wasn't in any real peril, he felt somewhat obligated in that it was very likely his fault they took her away.

More importantly, he'd never felt like he could actually be with anyone before, the way he felt about Dawn. Despite all his jokes and flirting, he did truly have feelings for her. The bus to Nashville took a good sixteen hours. It could have been done in a lot less time, but the bus stopped in every little town known to man. How was it possible? Every hour that passed Sunny found himself getting more anxious, a feeling which was new to him. He was used to feeling in control, even when he was completely alone.

Upon arriving in Nashville, he appreciated the reality that Dawn could still be anywhere within the state. He only had the name "Uncle Kemp" to go on. Sunny found a café with a free Wi-Fi sign, ordered a grilled ham and cheese sandwich and a coke and politely asked for the password. The waitress gave him the password and quickly walked away. For certain he smelled like Greyhound bus. That was never a good smell. He always met the strangest people with unique stories on Greyhound buses, but this time, he wasn't interested in chatting with anyone.

A few minutes later, Sunny's grilled ham and cheese arrived with his coke, a pile of Lay's potato chips, and a dill pickle. After immediately devouring the sandwich, chips, and pickles, he opened his smartphone and typed in cities in Tennessee. He made a list of the largest cities of Tennessee and did a person search for the name "Kemp." There were only 13 Kemps listed in Tennessee and one of them must be the uncle.

One by one he found phone number for 11 of the 13 Kemps. He hoped that Dawn's Uncle Kemp was not one of the 2 Kemps that didn't have a phone number.

One by one he crossed off Kemps from the list. One number belonged to a woodworking business, another to a dentist's office, another three were disconnected, and a sixth and seventh number appeared to be retirees. Sunny was feeling all but completely discouraged as he made it to the 11th number. When he dialed it, a man answered the phone and said, "Hello, Kemp here." Sunny hung up immediately. The area code proved to be in Gatlinburg. Gatlinburg it was, then. Sunny rented a room for the night, got some rest, and started off early the next morning for Gatlinburg. Another Greyhound and then a few local buses later, Sunny stepped off into Gatlinburg.

Chapter 8: Fate

While Sunny was searching the town for Dawn's uncle, Dawn herself was in despair. When would she see Sunny again? Could she return to the market? What about her dream of becoming a nurse? Was her family ever going to come back for her? Reality started to sink in that maybe her mother and father were not coming back for her. She was trapped in Gatlinburg, Tennessee. As Dawn began to panic, Sunny grew closer to finding her.

As fate would have it, finally in a local McDonald's a cashier knew the name Kemp and told him where the man lived. The worker told Sunny "Yeah, he's just a few miles away. I live in that direction and I can drop you off on the right road when my shift is over." "Thanks, that would be great. Name's Sunny, by the way," said Sunny. Two hours later Sunny was sitting in a stranger's car and growing closer to his destination.

Dawn was outside in the woods preparing a fire for the evening as the sun began to set. Her Uncle was inside, quiet as usual, preparing some sausages for the fire, when Sunny rounded the bend in the road. Dawn was startled as she recognized him, screamed, and jumped up.

Her Uncle came running, and found an equal surprise in recognizing what was transpiring. Sunny, the boy that his sister wanted to keep away from his niece, has somehow tracked her down to this unlikely location. Well, since the boy was here already, there was no sense in throwing him back into the street at night. They would of course have separate rooms on opposite sides of the house.

The three found themselves face to face in front of the fire. Uncle Kemp approached Sunny before Dawn did. "So, you must be Sunny," said Uncle Kemp. "Yessir," replied Sunny. Uncle Kemp started slowly "Well, as you can see, I'm not too keen on visitors, but since you're already here, you may as well have a sausage or two."

Dawn carefully and awkwardly wandered over to Sunny as they embraced fully—not to mention quickly, as not to upset their host and make him uncomfortable. "I assume you two understand I take no responsibility for Sunny being here. And he will not sleep in the same room as you. Meanwhile, I should notify your parents that he's here, but I don't think that will be necessary," stated Uncle Kemp.

Uncle Kemp bowed his head and went inside to give them a few moments of privacy. "How did you find me?" asked Dawn. "I'm an ex-foster kid, remember. I know how to find anyone and how to lose anyone," replied Sunny. "Right, of course," said Dawn. "Look, I don't know what to say. I like you a lot. And I don't know how I feel about being stuck here in Tennessee," continued Dawn. Sunny replied, "Well, it sounds like a pretty awful thing, but your folks do care about you, I'm sure. They just care about you in a way that doesn't make sense for you."

Dawn leaned her head on Sunny's shoulder. His body was warm, his voice was endearing, but he very much needed a shower. "Um, Sunny, let's talk after you bathe. What do you think?" asked Dawn. "Haha, of course," replied Sunny. He chuckled as Dawn asked her Uncle if Sunny could shower. While Sunny cleaned himself, Uncle

Kemp left a clean pair of jeans and a plaid button-down shirt on the sink for him to wear.

To Uncle Kemp, Sunny seemed all right. Dawn and Sunny reminded him of when he was a kid. Kids want to be able to experiment in relationships. It's hard in today's world to keep an Amish kid within the confines of being Amish. After Sunny rejoined the fire the three sat together, lost in their thoughts. What they would do? Sunny and Dawn may care for each other a lot, but they had quite the decision to make, and soon. Uncle Kemp reluctantly told them his story about how he ended up living on his own. He told them about the English girl he fell in love with when he was 18. He told them it was their decision to make.

The fire dimmed and no logs were added to the dying embers. The night was not their friend, explained Uncle Kemp. He didn't believe in staying outside without the fire. The night belongs to evil. "We go inside," he said. Uncle Kemp showed Sunny where he could sleep.

Chapter 9: Dawn

Dawn arrived in a peculiar way. The sun rose quietly, the sky lit up with yellows, blue and even a little bit of orange. When the morning came, it seemed like there was no easy decision to make. There wasn't. Dawn could try to reconnect with her family, or she could stay and start over with Sunny. It was evident that Uncle Kemp was not going to stop them from making their own decision.

"Good morning, Dawn!" chanted Sunny. Sunny started singing and dancing circles around Dawn. As she laughed he pulled her into his arms and kissed her lightly on the lips. "Would you like to come with me? We can go anywhere we want," said Sunny with great optimism.

"I don't know, Sunny. We hardly know each other. You're a good boy, a good man, but I think we both have decisions to make." Dawn was trying to be even-handed and rational. Sunny tried to meet her halfway. "Let's do this, then. Let's go home. Ask your parents' permission to date me. We'll tell them everything. If they accept, that's great. If they don't, you have to decide what life you want for yourself, Dawn. Don't let them hold you back from anything. Be who you are," implored Sunny.

By 10am the two were packed and ready to leave with Uncle Kemp's blessing. He dropped them both at the highway with their backpacks and wished them the best. Since he was a man of few words, his last sentence was only one: "Godspeed."

Dawn and Sunny both nodded and found their way back to the center of Galinburg. Soon they were at the Greyhound station once more. A few hot dogs from a food truck proved to be enough to fill their stomachs as they made their way to Nashville. In Nashville, they decided to press forward through the night on an overnight bus. The whole way Dawn and Sunny found themselves engaged in pleasant conversation. Sunny admitted that he had a gun, but it was only to defend himself. Dawn needed no more explanations, only peace, time, and patience. She fell asleep in his arms on the bus as it rolled along through the night.

They washed themselves at Sunny's house in the morning and planned to go to her parents' house the next morning at dawn, for which she was well named. Dawn knocked on the door with Sunny next to her side. The door opened and she said, "Hi Mom. This is Sunny. He is my boyfriend. If you can accept us both, we'd like to come inside."

AMISH BROKEN

GILLIAN BROWN

The Broken

Chapter 1

Job sauntered wordlessly down the winding dirt road, breathing in the cool moist air. May was his favorite month of the year for the way the impossibly green grass gave off a florid tangy smell, and the way smatterings of fluted white flowers blossomed in the nearby pasture. Every May, the world looked young again. Tiny calves learned to use their wobbly legs, and chicks lined up behind their mothers, before dunking themselves in the nearby pond. In May, many of their harvests grew up to seven feet, reaching skyward like tanned hands in silent prayer.

The world seemed so alive around Job and all of nature seemed to hum in a collective symphony of sound. The English who surrounded his small Amish community all had different names for God, but virtually all humans expressed a least a little wonder at these small miracles of nature. Job stopped in his tracks and watched in breathless wonder as a tiny doe hobbled across the road, struggling to balance on its new wiry legs. Job's heart softened at the sight of the little animal as he said a tiny prayer for its safety.

He hefted his fishing pole onto his shoulder and continued to walk the length of the long road.

In the Amish community, there were many festivals and celebrations during the month of May. Mothers would busy themselves sowing white wedding gowns, and the community would pull together to enjoy all the milestones of new life. If only his wife Laura were still alive, she'd be scurrying around with the rest of the ladies, enjoying all that Spring had to offer. Perhaps she too would have partaken in the maypole, as the ladies danced and weaved around one another, covering the pole in beautiful decorations.

Had Laura not died in childbirth, their baby would be 4 years old just this month. Job vaguely wondered what turns this would have caused his life to take. Soggy diapers and late night feedings would have certainly given way to the boy's membership in the church. Together they would have tilled the grainy fields from sun-up to sun-down, simultaneously clearing the land while remaking it, reclaiming it as their own. Job would have surely guided and instructed his son's young mind all the while. Yet, now both Laura and the baby were long gone. He squinted and silently prayed that they were both in heaven.

Even now, four years later, Job often woke in the dead of night and reached out for Laura after having a nightmare, only to find that his hands grasped only emptiness. That was the only way he could adequately describe his life without Laura: empty. There were no more sounds of her singing softly to herself in the kitchen as she baked. No more errant orange peels in the bedsheets. Laura's habit of eating oranges in bed used to make him angry, but now he missed it.

Job had long ago accepted that death was an inevitable part of life's design. Yet, still whenever he thought about his deceased wife and son, his heart grew heavy with longing. Laura had loved him so perfectly, and since her death, he hadn't even felt even a spark of feeling for anyone else, including himself. It was as though he now moved through life like a ghost, with one foot already in the afterlife. Try as he might, he neglected himself—no longer finding any reason to keep himself in good physical shape. Sometimes he neglected to eat for days.

Perhaps, Laura had been his one true soulmate. Perhaps, there was no coming back from that gravity of loss.

While Job was glad that they'd even met at all, he wondered about the loneliness that would surely cloud the rest of his life. His hopes of becoming a long-time husband and father, were destroyed the night that Laura had lay in their bedroom, screaming as she tried to push their baby out into the world. Her blood curdling screams could probably be heard a mile away as Job repeatedly asked the midwife what was wrong.

After ignoring him for a long while, the midwife finally admitted that the baby was stuck. "Can you pull him out?" Job asked. The midwife's gown was covered in Laura's blood, and she's reached her hands deep into the woman and yanked with all her might as Laura howled in pain. Then, she tried a second time. Again, Laura let out a shriek that could have woken the dead.

"We should make haste to the hospital!" Job said, throwing all caution aside. "There's no time for that!" The midwife shouted, looking down at the huge pool of blood spreading rapidly beneath Laura's rear. "Grab me a towel and a hot poker! Hurry! This is the only way that we can save her."

While Laura had bled to death, their baby had finally passed out of her birth canal. The midwife had handed the dead blue child to Job, while she urged Laura to hold on. Job stood there in shock, imagining the impossibly blue fingers and toes. Then, he wrapped his child in a blanket and rushed to Laura's side.

Job had replayed the scene countless times over the years. Always chiding himself for not having followed his instincts. He should have hefted her small frame into their coach and set off for the hospital. He should have realized that Laura was in trouble much earlier. There were so many things he blamed himself for, so many small decisions that had led to the death of both his wife and their baby.

When all was said and done, the midwife did all she could, but it wasn't enough. Job held tightly to Laura's hand as she passed out of this world and into the next.

The weeks that followed went by in a haze. The Amish community raised funds for the funerals. Church services and prayer meetings were held. Yet, each night, Job returned to the same now silent house, where he drew his fingers across Laura's pillow as he wailed, sometimes smelling the linen to re-capture the scent of her hair. He'd taken care to donate the baby's rocker and bassinet to a local charity—items which he'd spent hours crafting with his own hands. Then, he shut the door to the baby's room and that part of his life forever. He closed the door to his heart right along with it.

Chapter 2

Lina woke slowly. After three years of dating countless men she'd met online, after disastrous blind setups orchestrated by her well-meaning girlfriends, and many other more random encounters, she'd somehow managed to find her prince charming. Joe wasn't much to look at. In fact, most women wouldn't swoon over Joe or even take notice when he entered the room, but he'd been kind to her. Kinder than anyone had ever been.

Lina was a self-made woman, and she prided herself on that. After high school she'd been accepted into Aspen College, and had worked day and night to afford her classes. Somehow, she'd managed to pull it off and graduated with a decent G.P.A.

Shortly after that, she moved to Cleveland to start her own Marketing Business. There, she slaved away as an Intern for the Brown & Brown agency in the hopes of finding a permanent position there.

One day, they sent her on a short errand to Dr. Joe Dougan's Animal Hospital, who was seeking a new marketing firm to manage their public relations. Joe worked there as a vet at the time and was the owner. While Lina moved about, taking photos of the animal hospital, she'd been impressed by his total dedication to the cats and dogs entrusted into his care. He handled each and every one with tremendous gentleness and care.

One week later, her marketing firm had sent her back to capture some photos of Dr. Joe Dougan's work with a nearby pet rescue that had just liberated over two-hundred dogs from a nearby breeding farm. Some of the dogs looked beyond all hope, yet Dr. Dougan refused to give up on them.

Lina lost her heart when together they'd opened up a small cardboard box, only to find a tiny whimpering beagle puppy inside. The dog's snout was covered in mud, and his fur was littered with fleas, yet Dr. Joe Dougan refused to give up on the little guy. When they learned that the puppy was so young he'd need to be hand-fed from an eye-dropper every few hours, Joe's heart sunk. No one in his office had time for such an undertaking, which meant that the puppy would probably die.

Lina swallowed. "I'll do it," she said, without hesitation, placing the camera down on the counter. Only seconds later, she found herself stroking the tiny pup, who fit easily into the palm of her hand. The puppy cried the entire drive back to her apartment, and she'd taken great care to make him a nest of old blankets and pillowcases, which she propped up on her bed, right beside where she slept. Gradually, as the weeks passed, he grew stronger and more vivacious—eventually becoming quite naughty.

A few days later, when Lina woke and the puppy was missing, she panicked. He was so tiny; it wasn't as though he could have gone far. She checked the front door, which was locked, and beneath all the furniture, but he wasn't there. When Lina found him curled up beneath one of her potted plants, she grabbed her camera, snapped a few photos, and officially gave him the name Potts.

As time droned by, the notion of ever parting with Potts became intolerable, and so Lina went back to Dr. Joe and formally adopted him. "How much is the adoption fee?" Lina had asked. "How about one date tonight at a nice restaurant? I'll pay." Dr. Joe had smartly replied.

From that day forth, Lina and Potts were inseparable. No matter where Lina went, Potts was close on her heels and today was no exception.

Joe had asked for her hand in marriage just three months ago. Lina had answered with a resounding yes, as Joe popped open a ring case, inside which a huge diamond glistened. She could scarcely believe that anyone could be so perfect.

Today was the day of their wedding, and Lina felt like the luckiest girl in all the world.

All her friends and family were in attendance, and everyone seemed overjoyed for both of them. Even Potts was there, donning a white doggy suit, while gnawing at a squeak toy on the floor. Though, he seemed unusually tense.

Lina reached down to pat him on the head, while her hairdresser worked to curl her hair into spirals. Another woman gently applied makeup to her face at the same time, and the room was abuzz as her mother and bridesmaids got ready. She felt nervous, but her heart was also filled with love. She was marrying the kindest man she'd ever known.

A few hours later, Lina stood arm and arm with her father, as they prepared to walk down the aisle. Everyone else was already seated in the church, bustling with anxiousness. Lina breathed in deep, waiting for the double-doors of the church to open, when someone urgently tapped her on the back.

Lina paused and looked up at a man dressed a black suit, her body immediately seized by horror. The doors to the church swung open, and all her friends and family beamed at her, looking upon her with smiles on their faces. Then, Lina felt the cuffs clamp down around her wrists as the FBI agent pulled her away by the elbow to the squad car which waited outside.

"What is the meaning of this!" Her father screamed. "Lina Edwards, you are under arrest for murder in the first degree. You have the right to remain silent..." The agent read her rights to her, and she was in a state of total shock and incredible humiliation.

All her friends and family's smiles turned to horror, as they watched he escorted from the building, still wearing her wedding dress, and stuffed her into the back of a police car. What was supposed to be the happiest day of her life, had quickly turned into a nightmare. Yet, little did Lina know that the real nightmare had scarcely begun.

Chapter 3

Lina was led into an interrogation room for questioning. She was all but thrown into a metal chair in front of a one-sided plate glass window. They left her inside the freezing room for hours, and then finally returned with stacks of folders containing evidence.

A female agent tossed a photo down onto the table. The picture appeared to be that of a body that had been skinned alive, though the head and hands were chopped off. Lina took one look at the phone and vomited on the floor.

"You want to explain why this was inside your storage unit downtown?" The agent asked.

Lina's jaw dropped and she feared she might vomit. "How about this one? You want to explain this one to me?" The agent slammed down a second photograph of a woman who appeared to have died by strangulation. Lina squinted at the photo. The woman was wearing a sweater, *her* sweater—a sweater that Joe had asked her if he could take to the Goodwill over a month ago.

After hours and hours of interrogation, Lina finally understood that the FBI had no real intentions of actually prosecuting her. They already had overwhelming evidence against Joe and knew that he was the real killer. They knew because many of the victims had been murdered through the administration of euthanasia drugs intended for cats and dogs; they knew because they'd found his semen all over the corpses; they knew because his fingerprints and hair fibers were all over the corpses.

The FBI simply needed some level of cooperation from her and wanted to communicate the seriousness of what might occur if she refused.

Shaking, Lina called her father to retain and attorney an signed FBI statements attesting to the origins of her sweater, and the fact that Joe had ready access to her storage unit. They already had him in custody in a nearby seclusion room. "As long as you don't flee the state, you're free to go," the agent said. "We'll probably still need you to testify though."

Lina stood up, still wearing her wedding dress and turned to go. "I'm sorry, Lina. I'm sorry we ruined your wedding, but wives can't be forced to testify against their husbands, so I hope you understand why we had to bring you in the moment we found out about this wedding. We needed to nab this guy, before he conned you into marrying him."

When the police car dropped her off at home, the place felt eerie and terrifying for the first time in her life. The police had searched the home and virtually everything was overturned and in total shambles.

All the things she'd worked so hard to build—all of it, had come crashing down in a single day. Potts greeted her at the door and she patted him on the head and then scooped the small dog up into her arms. Her dad had gratefully dropped Potts off less than an hour prior, and he wiggled in her arms, panting as she gave him a belly rub.

Suddenly, Lina looked around. There were photos of she and Joe all over the walls. His tennis shoes were on the floor, and one of his jackets was balled up on the sofa. Lina let out a wailing scream as she grabbed her car keys. With Potts still in her arms, she sprinted out of the house and into her red Mustang, ready to leave it all behind—consequences be damned.

Chapter 4

Potts leaned his head out of the passenger side window while Lina put the pedal to the metal. Enough was enough. Life had dealt her some terrible blows before, but this was by far the worst. This was an all-time low.

She'd almost married a serial killer? The thought simultaneously terrified and infuriated her. All those times she'd ran her fingers through his hair, comforted her with his body. Those same hands that had wandered all over her body with lust and adoration were also chopping peoples' head's off? The same hands that had so lovingly patted Potts on the head were also administering drugs to human beings that caused cardiac arrest, and eventually death.

The thought made her sick. She wasn't sure about what angered her more: the fact that he'd done such horrible things, or the fact that she'd never seen any of it coming. She felt dirty in her skin—as though he'd left a mark on her somehow.

Lina pressed down the accelerator as Potts leapt with excitement. She had no idea where she was even going—she just knew that she'd had enough. She'd helped Joe build his veterinary practice into a thriving chain, and this was the thanks she got. *Murderer*, she thought.

Tears brimmed in Lina's eyes as she sped down the country road, driving faster and faster. When the deer darted out in front of her car, there was no time to react.

The deer flew up onto the hood as she pulled the steering wheel hard to the right. Time seemed to stand still as the windshield shattered, and bits of broken glass sprayed all around her. Then, she was tumbling—the sound of screeching metal against the thud of the earth resounded over and over as the car made revolution after revolution, screeching as it toppled over itself. Lina reached over to where Potts had been sitting to grab him, and screamed as he flew out the busted window.

Chapter 5

The last thing Job had expected to find in the road was a screaming woman, wearing a wedding gown. There was blood all over her gown, but she didn't even seem to notice as he sprinted over to her. The woman was too busy looking beneath bushes and in large thickets. "Potts!" Lina screamed. "Potts!" She yelled, calling into the tall grass. When Job reached her side, she didn't even bother to explain the mangled car, or her odd attire. "He's a short dog. The car flipped and he fell out and it probably scared him to death," Lina cried, wiping away tears. "I have no idea if he's injured or anything! Please, help me." Lina sobbed.

Job placed a gentle hand on her shoulder, and then he dashed out into a nearby cornfield. While Lina screamed the dog's name over and over, Job lowered his ear and listened. Not far away, he could hear the jingling of what he imagined was Pott's collar and a high-pitched whimper. Without hesitation, Job took off in the direction of the sound, following it to its source.

Potts had made his way into a small clearing and was gnawing away at a cob of corn, crying intermittently. Job scooped the small dog up into his strong arms and checked him over for injuries. Luckily, he didn't even have a scratch.

"I've got him!" Job called as he made his way back to the hysterical woman, glancing at the dog's collar which read: *my name is Potts and I belong to Lina Edwards.*

Job turned the name over in his mind a few times, *Lina.*

When the woman saw her dog, her entire demeaner changed. She reached for him with outstretched arms and clasped him tightly to her chest as she sighed. Then, she let out a scream.

Job looked on at the odd scene. Here was a woman in a bloody wedding dress, clutching a dog, wailing hysterically at the top of her lungs. She was very obviously having some kind of mental break and seemed to be scarcely hanging on by a thread. Something about her eyes, made his heart soften. After all, he knew how terrifying it could be to feel assaulted by the world and totally alone.

That said, whatever had happened to Lina, seemed to be a matter for the other women—women's work—and so Job gently led her by the elbow down the dirt road toward he and his sister's farm. Poor Lina cried and wailed the entire way, and didn't even seem cognizant of the fact that they were walking. She just cried and cried.

Lina didn't even seem to notice what was happening, as Job's sister Ruth led her into their small guest bedroom in the back. Still clutching her dog Potts, Lina tucked herself into their guest bed while Ruth prepared a medicinal broth for her. Minutes after swallowing the concoction, Lina was fast asleep.

Chapter 6

The next morning, Job woke with a jolt, eager to check on the strange woman. Lina had slept soundly through the night, and Ruth had taken the liberty of helping Potts outside to do his business, offering him a bowl of chicken while Lina still dozed heavily. When the young woman did finally wake, hours later, she appeared in the kitchen, still standing there in her wedding gown, with her mascara having left huge black circles beneath her eyes.

"Well, it's good to see you're finally awake, darling." Ruth said, rushing to Lina's side. "I've prepared a lovely breakfast for you, so if you'd like to put on something more comfortable..." Job averted his eyes. The wedding gown was beautiful, but left little to the imagination. He felt his pulse quicken as he looked at her.

Lina looked down, seeming to realize that she was still wearing her blood wedding dress for the first time. She drew her arms up around herself in embarrassment, as Ruth jumped to her feet and led her back into the bedroom. A few minutes later, Ruth entered the kitchen where Job was already seated, wearing an Amish dress. "We'll have to patch that up," Job said, pointing to a scrape on Lina's arm.

Ruth passed a heaping bowl of biscuits to her brother Job, who then handed it to Lina. Lina pulled a biscuit off the pile and started hefting gravy on top. Everyone at the table watched in horror as Lina placed scoop after scoop of gravy onto the biscuit, not stopping until the plate overflowed onto the floor.

Job gave his sister Ruth a stern look from across the table. "Perhaps we should call the bishop," Ruth said in a low hush. Job nodded kindly.

"Is there anywhere we can take you? Do you have any family that we should call?" Ruth asked. Lina lowered her head and shook her head no. Then, she started to cry again.

"Why don't we get some fresh air. It always helps me to go for a nice walk in a field of flowers when I feel down and I think Potts would enjoy that too. What do you say?" Job asked, extending a warm hand in Lina's direction. He helped her up from the chair and led her out onto the porch.

Wordlessly, they descended the front steps and then began a slow stroll into the hilly country side. Job held tight to Potts' leash as he darted around, sniffing rocks and grass. For a long time they walked on in silence. The wind tousled Lina's hair, and for the first time, Job noticed that she was unspeakably beautiful. Her green eyes starkly contrasted against her jet-black hair and pale skin. She had full lips and high cheekbones. She was absolutely stunning.

Lina looked nothing like his wife Laura had, but still, there was something in her soul that kept drawing his eyes and pulling at his heart.

"Do you want to talk about it?" Job finally asked her after a long while. They'd rounded the cow pastures and were drawing closer to a small rose garden. Lina looked up at him, her searing green eyes studied his features. "You can't laugh at me," she said finally. "I don't make a habit of laughing at people's pain," Job answered without skipping a beat. Lina seemed to accept his answer and they moved into the brush a bit farther, before they spoke again.

"I was supposed to get married," Lina said after a while. Job nodded. "I gathered that from your wedding dress." Lina's eyes shot back to his. "The guy I was supposed to marry…I trusted him. I believed in him. I loved him." There was so much pain in her voice as she spoke. Job nodded, listening intently. "Was he unfaithful to you?" Job asked, wondering how any man could be unfaithful to such a beautiful and sensitive woman.

"Right before I was going to walk down the aisle, the FBI arrested me. Joe's been killing women. All this time, right under my nose, I was living with a murderer. He killed eight women that we know of." Lina said.

Her words lay heavy in the air for a long while. Lina had expected Job to run away screaming, but instead he nodded and hummed softly to himself. "Do you think people are born the way they are, or do you think life changes them into a better or worse version of themselves?" He asked her after a long while. It wasn't what she'd expected him to say. "I wish I knew the answer," Lina said quietly.

For the first time, Lina noticed his strong hands and muscled arms. She admired his gentleness with Potts, and couldn't help but sneak a few peeks at his muscular thighs, which were only barely contained by the fabric of this pants. It was his silent strength that she liked the most. For some reason, her presence made her feel protected.

"The only thing I know, is that I would never choose to be a murderer." Lina said, after a long time. Job nodded. "Nor would I," he added.

As they drew closer to the grove, he pulled a rose free and then slowly closed her hand around it. A feeling of warmth moved through her body like a shockwave. She ran her fingers over the thorn, and then lifted the petals to her nose, drinking in the strong sweet smell.

"Would you like to know what I thought, when my wife and son died?" Job asked her. Lina gasped. She'd had no idea that this quiet soft-spoken gentleman had suffered through something so terrible. In her mind, she'd always fantasized that the Amish led idyllic and perfect lives, that tragedy never struck their homes or communities. Now, she realized how foolish her assumption had been. "I'm sorry for your loss," Lina said after a long while and Job nodded.

"It took me a long time to accept that the world isn't just or fair—certainly not in the way we want it to be. Terrible things happen to the best of people. After my son died, I went to our Amish library and I started to read up on all the people that die of starvation every day. The number was well over 20,000." He said. "Why is it that billions of good people allow over 20,000 people to die of hunger every day. That means that billions of people choose to look the other way, each and every day."

"I wasn't looking the other way with my fiancé," Lina shot back—mistaking his comment for a slight. "If I'd have known that Joe was hurting people, I would have put a stop to it." Job nodded. "I can tell that about you—that you're a helper of mankind." Job swallowed.

"So, let me tell you what I learned after my family died. I realized that in this life, you're never actually grieving alone. No matter what happens to you, someone somewhere else on the planet is hurting with you, at the very same exact time as you are." He said, his brown eyes filled with emotion.

Lina sighed deeply, feeling a little bit of relief. Somehow, his words made a little of her pain subside. They sat down in the field and Job placed his arm around her and drew her close. He could feel the soft rise of her breath, and her skin was impossibly soft against his. The wind blew a bit of her dark hair onto his shoulder and he let it stay there—breathing in the smell of her shampoo. Then, Lina slowly leaned her head over on Job's shoulder and fell asleep.

Chapter 7

When Job and Lina returned from their stroll, Ruth was stressed out and flitting about, panicked. "The media has been calling my phone all afternoon!" Ruth called from the porch. "You have a phone?" Lina asked, looking to Job who nodded.

The local news' station had dubbed the situation *Doctor Dougan's House of Horrors*, and everyone wanted to get some kind of interview with Lina. CNN and FoxNews were willing to pay top dollar for just fifteen minutes of her time. How they'd even managed to find out that she had fled to the Amish was unknown.

"I do need money," Lina said softly, as she picked up the phone. Job walked over and gently took it from her. He laid it back down into its holster on the counter. "You should never do anything, just for the money," he said. "Only do things that you believe in." His eyes were filled with gentle fire, and Lina couldn't help but want to kiss him right there. Perhaps she could drown her troubles in his strong muscled body. She imagined how good it might feel to lay in his arms as he kissed her with his soft rounded lips. Lina's heart quickened, yet it was the sound of Ruth's voice which brought her back out of her daydream.

"We'll need to make sure we handle all of this in accordance with our religious laws," Ruth said to Lina, as she flipped through a handwritten telephone book to find the bishop's phone number.

Very quickly, Ruth called their Amish bishop over for his advice.

Lina sat quietly in the living room as the elderly gentleman looked her up and down. "This woman is in need of our help," Job said. The Bishop nodded thoughtfully. "Are you a woman of good moral character?" The bishop asked Lina.

"My fiancé killed a bunch of people," Lina answered flatly. The bishop nodded. "I've heard that unfortunate truth from both the police and the people around here, but what about you? What about you being separate from him?" Lina considered his words for a moment and then looked over at Job. "I'm nothing like my fiancé," she said finally, and that was that.

"Good then," the Bishop said, standing up. "You will stay here with Job and his sister Ruth as long as you need to. We will show the world what it means to be Amish, what it means to be kind...and how our way is the way of peace."

The bishop calmly strode from the room, leaving a smiling Job in his wake.

Chapter 8

Days turned into weeks and weeks grew into months. Job looked on as Lina transformed from a shy traumatized woman, to someone who often danced in the cornfield, or went swimming in the creek when she thought no one was watching. One day, Job had followed her and had smiled as she dove head-first into the water, fully clothed.

He pranked her by diving in after her, saying "boo!" loudly when she surfaced. At first, Lina had been angry, but her displeasure soon gave way to hearty laughter.

Watching Lina come back into herself was like watching a dead flower blossom back to life. Job watched her with both wonderment and amazement as she marveled at even the smallest things. The more time passed, the more it seemed as though her spirit was slowly returning. She was developing so many skills—doing so many things she'd previously thought were impossible.

Once a city girl and a marketer, Lina was not riding horses and wrangling escapee chickens. She helped mend the broken fences, and learned the work of the farm.

Lina rose early in the morning to help Ruth tend to the cows, and had learned to churned butter. Ruth grew increasingly fond of her and often bragged about her budding abilities in the kitchen.

As Lina became well, she also started attending community events. There were so many weddings and celebrations within their community, and while the Amish worked hard, they also believed in experiencing the simple joys of life. She'd learned the names of everyone in their township and often asked how folks were doing, remembering even the most minute details, which made Job beam with pride.

Lina had even started to learn cheese making too. During her first batch, she proudly went out to the cow pasture and worked hard, pulling at the large cow's udders. The cow, Bessie, responded by mooing loudly, and immediately kicking over the bucket of milk.

During Lina's second cheese-making attempt, she'd thrown out the curds and kept the glossy liquid, while her new Amish friends chuckled beneath their breath. Then, after realizing her mistake, she tried to dig the curds out of the rubbish and ended up with cheese that had old rose blossoms in it, which they let harden and ate anyway. Surprisingly, it was delicious. On Lina third attempt, everything ran smoothly...yet now she always put a dash of rose petals in.

One night, while Lina and Job sat on the porch, staring up into the starry night sky, Job was surprised when Lina reached for his hand. "Thank you for everything you did for me," Lina said softly. "Well, it was easy. You are easy to love, "Job responded. Lina squeezed his hand in the darkness and warmth vaulted through her body like electricity. She had so many feelings for him, but struggled to put them into words. She'd wanted to say the words, *I love you, Job*, but simply couldn't.

In his own quiet way, Job had expressed his love, and Lina knew that it came from a place of truth and deep caring. She remembered that day on the road, when she'd been panicked—screaming Potts' name after her Mustang had wrecked.

Job had been so calm and loving in the way he'd gently looked for Potts, and returned to her with the frightened dog curled up in his arms. He'd taken the both of them into his home without a single question asked, and had treated her like family. It was something she would never forget. It was a kindness so great she would never be able to repay it.

"Have I ever told you that I think you're beautiful?" Job asked her. The words were a shock to her ears. His hand gently rested over where it rested on her thigh. Lina moaned gently. "I think that each time you touch me Job, you make my spirit anew." Lina whispered. He brought his hand up and stroked her hair while he stared deeply into her green eyes. Then, time seemed to stand still as he leaned in and pressed his lips against hers—a feeling that brought so much pleasure rushing through her body, she felt as though she might pass out.

"Don't stop," Lina said breathlessly, as Job withdrew. "If I don't stop now, I might not stop for the rest of my life." Job said softly, and then squeezed her hand again.

Even better, as time passed Lina became more active in the community and in the church. As she learned their ways, making cheese and butter from scratch became less of a chore and more an art-form. Lina started to take pride in the things she accomplished, and at the end of the day, when she climbed into bed, she slept soundly, as though all was well again.

The next morning, Job asked her if she'd be willing to accompany him to a prayer group.

Lina looked over at Job's dark eyes. He was such a handsome man, but more striking was his wisdom and depth of character. While not many words passed between them, Lina was reaching a point where she could scarcely imagine her life without Job. She was willing to go anywhere with him—anywhere.

She enjoyed spending her evenings sitting beside him, as they read aloud. Sometimes he'd talk to her about plans he had for new shed designs, or new animals to purchase. Their lives were simple, yet pure.

"Lina...have you ever thought about...well, about the rest of your life?" Job asked tentatively. "What do you mean?" Lina asked. Job cleared his throat. "Well, you've made a life here with us. Do you like your new life?" He asked.

Lina sighed, with tears brimming in her eyes. "I like it very much." She answered. "Do you like me?" Job asked her. Lina turned to him with tears streaking down her face. "More than words could ever express. More than anything." She said. Job smiled kindly, taking her hand. "Then, will you do me the honor of spending the rest of your life with me? I can't imagine living even one second without you. I'm so sorry for all the hardships you've faced, but I promise to try and help you feel better."

"You already have," Lina said quietly. "And anyway, I'm grateful for all those hardships because they brought me to you. Yes, I'll marry you." She blurted out, sobbing with happiness. "I'm so grateful for everything that brought me to you."

Job moved towards her and wrapped her in his arms. Again, he looked deeply into her eyes. Somehow, two broken people had made each other whole again.

The End.

AMISH ROSE

SABRINA VICKS

42

Chapter 1: Saying Goodbye

She pictured a flower, however, instead of it blooming towards the sun, it folded inward, protecting the center. She and her daughters were the center and it would stay that way for a year when people would come to her dwelling every Sunday to sit with the family in mourning. For a year they would adorn themselves in the appropriate black attire and show nothing on their faces, no feelings, no tears. At least for that last part she would not have to pretend.

For three days, she would tend to her duties knowing that his grave was getting deeper. The body was prepared as was the coffin—simply and cleanly, in accordance with tradition. People from all over the community came to the viewings—first at their home, then at the funeral, and finally, at the gravesite where his body was laid to rest. She did not struggle through the proceedings because unlike other funerals she had heard of where the family and friends gather around and tell stories of remembrance and honor of the deceased, all she had to do was muster enough energy to thank the Lord. Which she did with all of her heart because she was truly thankful.

Once the last of the visitors left her home, she felt as if for the first time in a long time her lungs could actually fill with air. A great deal of pressure had been released from her chest and she no longer felt as though the world were rolling on top of her—but it had nothing to do with mourning the loss of her husband and everything to do with finally being able to rejoice it with no eyes on her to witness the impropriety. She was no longer Rebecca the married, she was now Rebecca the widow.

"Mama," her youngest daughter, Sarah, called out to her from the door frame. She was dressed in her long white nightgown with her simple bonnet covering her long, raven black hair. Her mother often wondered where her daughter got her striking beauty and she often felt as though she may envy her a little too. Such a pure beauty—she could not be missed unlike her mother who was easily overlooked in a crowd. "Mama?" Sarah said quietly, taking a few steps toward her mother.

"Yes, Sarah. I'm awake, it's alright. Come sit by me," Sarah snuggled in close to her mother and rested her head in the small crook her mother made between her arm and stomach. "You should be asleep now."

"I know, mama. I just couldn't sleep," her eight-year-old daughter glanced up at her with her clear blue eyes and her mother saw them as two pools of untainted honesty.

"I could not sleep, either" Rebecca confessed. "What thoughts do you have in your mind that are disturbing your sleep?"

"Every time I close my eyes, I see the men lowering him into the grave and he reaches the bottom. But when I look into the grave to say goodbye, the coffin is open and he is not inside," Sarah looked into the distance as she recounted her nightmares, "I'm afraid."

"It is normal, Sarah, for a daughter to miss her father once he has left this earth. We just have to remind ourselves that this was the Lord's plan and while we may not always understand it, we must always have faith in it. We must always stay true to Him and thank Him for his blessings."

"I am not sad, mama," Sarah whispered quietly, "I'm afraid he will come back." Her mother looked down at her daughter knowingly and she sighed—not out of frustration or impatience—out of an indescribable silence that her daughter had to endure her first eight years in such a way that she would be afraid of her dead father.

"I understand, Sarah. He won't be coming back, I promise you that. Once he died, his soul left his body and a body cannot move or breathe on its own. It must have the soul in order to live," Rebecca paused. She felt too tired to get into a lecture on life and death so she added this, "This is why it is important for us to protect and preserve the integrity of our souls." Sarah nodded sleepily as she wiped at her eyes. "Go to sleep, Sarah. We have to start anew tomorrow and we must be at our best."

Sarah got up and walked down the short hallway to her room which she shared with her sister, Ruby. Rebecca heard Sarah climb into bed and mumble something quietly to herself.

Rebecca stayed where she was and recalled the last few months. She looked down at her arm and pulled up the sleeve of her dress to reveal the dark bruise just above her elbow. Fingers wrapped around her arm forcing her into her place. *It is ironic*, she thought, *the man who gave me this is gone but the bruises still remain.* She pulled down her sleeve again and looked out the window to the spot in the garden where she merited such a reaction.

"Rebecca!" Tom yelled from the top step of the house.

"Yes, Tom?" She wiped the sweat from her brow as she stood up from her garden bed. The sun was beating down with such force that she could feel each breath turn hot against her lips as soon as she exhaled. She watched as her husband came over to where she was standing and she could tell from the way he pulled his eyebrows together and twitched up the right side of his mouth that he was unhappy with something. "Girls," Rebecca said to her two daughters, "mind the rest of the rows, please. I need to go inside to talk with your father."

"Do you need help?" Ruby asked, peering over her shoulder at her father's expression.

"Young lady, did you hear what your mama told you to do?" her father spoke quietly, but he was the very definition of a calm before a storm.

"Yes, sir. Sorry, sir." Ruby and Sarah turned back to the garden and continued their work as their mother walked inside following their father.

"Would you like some water, Tom?" Rebecca asked her husband.

"No," he stared out into the garden and watched the two girls working. "Those girls are lazy and they are not fulfilling their duties as respectable women."

"Tom, they are eight and ten years old. They work hard every day helping me around the house to clean and make sure food is prepared when you come home. They have been in the garden with me all day despite how hot it is today."

"This is just like you," he scoffed, "you are always making excuses for them! How can you expect them to grow up when you are always there to coddle them?"

"I am not coddling them, I—" Tom directed his glare at Rebecca and she froze midsentence. This is it, she had somehow pushed him to this point again and he was not going to let her walk out of here without learning a lesson his way. He reached toward her and grabbed her by the arm, pressing down so hard that she could already feel her fingers tingling from lack of blood flow. "Tom, please. I understand. I will make them work harder. I promise you!"

"They have learned laziness from your example. If you ever desire our daughters to succeed, you need to fix yourself first." He released her arm and took another small step forward so that his nose rested softly against her own. "You reap what you sew, Rebecca. Never forget that."

His words lingered in her mind and Rebecca snapped open her eyes and slowly realized that she had fallen asleep thinking about the exhausting events over the past few days. She blew out the candle and to the night air she said, "Goodbye, Tom."

Chapter 2: The Healing

The girls woke up in the morning and came to the breakfast table where they began preparing their usual morning cereals and oatmeal. Rebecca woke a bit later than she was used to and she was surprised to find the girls working so efficiently with no supervision.

"Well, good morning girls. It seems as though you have all gotten a good night rest," Rebecca said pleasantly as she prepared her own breakfast meal.

"Didn't you sleep well, mama?" Ruby asked, "I know I did for the first time in a long time." Rebecca looked at her eldest child and although she shared the same black hair as her sister, Ruby was plainer than Sarah. She had small freckles which lined her nose and thin lips stretched across her face. But despite her looks, Ruby was a sharp young girl and she often sounded and acted more mature than any of the other girls her age.

"I slept well," Rebecca conceded and she caught a sideways glance from Sarah prior to continuing, "Today we will have to tend to the livestock and we will also have to start harvesting our crops."

"Mama, when we are finished working, can I go to play with Mary? She's invited me to go down by the river with her to read."

"You may, Ruby," Rebecca nodded at her daughter and then added, "Bring Sarah with you." Sarah looked at her mother and then at Ruby who just shrugged her shoulders and kept eating.

"Mama, are you sure you want to be alone?" Sarah finally asked.

"It will be okay, Sarah. We will focus on our tasks for the day and keep our minds prayerful and everything will be okay." Ruby looked between her mother and sister not fully understanding the conversation taking place, but she decided not to bother trying to examine it further than face value.

The days turned into months and their harvest was growing steadily. The hard work provided a welcome distraction for Rebecca and her girls as they all tried to move forward with their lives.

The day was much cooler than when they had planted the crops so the work did not seem as difficult. The women worked hard with few breaks in order to complete their tasks efficiently. Once it was time to check the livestock and feed them, Rebecca told the girls that they could go meet with Mary. She watched as the girls skipped happily with each other, hand in hand, towards the direction of the river.

Rebecca finished tending to her livestock and she went back into the house. It was still early in the morning and she had already finished a great deal of work. While she sat there, she couldn't help but feel a bit sad about losing Tom. He was not the most righteous man in the entire world, but he tried to have the best intentions. Rebecca recalled memories which were much sweeter when he began to court her, oh how he had made her smile. Now all of her memories are muddled together in a dark grey matter and she cannot decide what to feel anymore.

In that moment, with her girls gone to the river, Rebecca decided to go to a service away from her own community. She needed fresh faces and above all, she needed space. Space to talk with the Lord and be honest with herself and with Him about what she was feeling about her whole situation. She felt good, but the guilt that came with that was almost overwhelming and she needed the peace that only He could provide.

She went outside and hooked up the buggy. She drove it outside of her own small community, waving at the people who noticed her and keeping her eyes forward. It wasn't that far to the nearest community and she hoped that being away from it all would help her to gain some much-needed perspective.

As she pulled into the community, she leaned out of her buggy to a young woman walking past her carrying a pail of water. "Excuse me," she called out to the passerby. The young woman glanced at her and smiled.

"You're not from here, are you?" she asked Rebecca.

"No," Rebecca replied sheepishly, "I come from the community very near to here. I just wanted to—well, I was wondering if you could point me in the direction to the nearest service."

"I am headed there myself, feel free to follow me."

Rebecca offered to give the woman a ride to the house, and she climbed in beside Rebecca pointing the way to the house where the service was to be held that morning. The son of the house came out to greet the woman whose name Rebecca learned was Emma.

"I'm sorry," the boy apologized as his cheeks reddened from embarrassment, "I can't seem to remember your name."

"She's new here, Eli. You do not need to be ashamed!" Emma exclaimed with a friendly smile.

"Oh!" Eli said, clearly relieved. He offered to take her horse into the stable while the women went inside to talk amongst themselves before the service began.

Emma walked ahead of Rebecca and introduced her to all the women in the house. Finally, they came to Eli's mother, Naomi, who was hosting today's service. "Hello, Emma," the woman pulled her in for a quick hug, "and who do we have here?"

"Hello, my name is Rebecca. I come from the community near to here and I wanted to come for a service," she explained.

"We are all happy you could join us!" Naomi said, "Is your husband with the other men?"

Rebecca paused a moment before responding. She knew this was already a strange situation for a woman from another community to come all the way here for a service and she did not want to get into a conversation regarding her newly appointed status as a widow, so she replied, "I am not married."

"Ah," the woman said, looking at Rebecca up and down. She smiled but it did not reach her eyes and Rebecca knew that the other women in the group would start forming their own opinions about her now. She had just wanted to get away from the eyes that knew her sad story, but now she found herself amongst eyes that assumed her sad story, which felt even worse.

Rebecca walked over to a bench where Emma sat and the service soon began. The first preacher stood in front of the community and began speaking.

"Trust in the Lord with all your heart and lean not on your own understanding. These are the words that we read in Proverbs, but do we truly live by them?" he asked, "Can we consider ourselves righteous and people of faith if we only read words and do not act on them or incorporate them into our own daily lives? No, those of us who do not believe in the Lord's plan, we cannot claim to be righteous. Those of us who believe only in our own selves, our own hearts, our own minds—we forget that these do not belong to us alone. They belong to everyone, they belong to Him. We are all part of his plan and the Lord will giveth and taketh away as His will commands. Whether we understand—rather, whether we choose to try to understand, this is where we fail."

Rebecca glanced around the room at all the bobbing heads who were taking in the words with open minds and open hearts. She closed her eyes and reflected on her own situation and in the deepest corners of her heart, she felt relief. She decided in this moment, that she should not feel unhappy or guilty—the Lord's plan took Tom from her life for a reason. The Lord's plan gave her comfort and a chance at finding happiness again. Although she did not understand it, she would never fully understand it, she knew in this moment that she did not need to.

Chapter 3: The Meeting

The end of the service came around and the men and women separated to enjoy their meals and reflect on the words spoken.

Emma walked next to Rebecca as they found a place on the benches to sit and talk together. "How did you enjoy the service?" Emma asked.

"It was exactly what I needed to hear," Rebecca replied, smiling. "The Lord certainly does work in mysterious ways." Emma nodded in agreement. "Emma, I must share something with you about earlier."

"What is it?" Emma asked her new friend.

"When I was speaking with the woman earlier, I told her that I was not married. While that is technically true, it is not the whole truth," Emma pulled her eyebrows together as a puzzled look came across her face. Rebecca continued, "I was married. My husband, he—well, he passed away a few months ago. I have two beautiful young daughters that I cherish with all of my heart, but I needed to go to a place on my own to listen to my heart and hear what the Lord needed me to hear."

"Oh my," Emma said, reaching for Rebecca's hand, "well as the sermon said today, the Lord giveth and taketh away as His will commands. So, we should thank Him for his undying presence in our lives making all things possible for us through Him."

Rebecca smiled kindly at her new friend, sincerely feeling happy that she had the chance to meet Emma. The two women finished their meal and offered to help hand out the coffee and iced water to all the members. As she walked around offering the beverages among the men, she caught the eye of one man sitting on a bench talking with the son that Rebecca had met earlier.

"Rebecca!" Eli called out to her. She walked over to where he was sitting and offered him a drink. "No, thank you. I have water already. Have you met Jacob yet?"

"No, I have not." Rebecca looked over at the man sitting on the bench and she could feel her face growing warmer as she took in his tanned face and his respectfully groomed deep brown beard. But what struck here even more were his green eyes—they reminded her of spring and grass and fresh, healthy crops, and the innocence of childhood when everything seemed possible.

The man coughed quietly bringing Rebecca back to the present. "I said it is nice to meet you. Where are you from?" He smiled at her tenderly causing her face to turn red once more.

Eli answered for her, "She is from a community near to here. Emma knows her!"

"Ah," the man responded, "Emma is my youngest sister."

Rebecca finally unfroze and managed to say, "Yes." He looked at her quizzically and then she quickly added, "I mean yes, I am from a community near to here. And yes, I met Emma today. She is a beautiful woman who has helped me in many ways already."

"Yes, she has a keen ability of getting along well with everyone." Rebecca smiled at the man and then he added, "Well, I don't want to keep you from your duties much longer. It was nice meeting you."

"Right, of course. Thank you!" Rebecca walked away from their bench and headed back inside to the kitchen where she placed the pitchers. She found Emma in the kitchen already, waiting for her.

"Emma, I've just met your brother, Jacob. He was very kind."

Emma smiled warmly, "Yes, he is the best brother. He always helps me when I need it and it seems he cannot say no to me!" She laughed at her own private joke.

Rebecca looked down at her feet, for some reason the comment Emma made felt too intimate to share with someone that she had just met. She looked back up to find Emma toiling with the pitchers as she prepared a new coffee. "Well," Rebecca started, "I suppose I should get going. I do not want to leave my daughters for much longer. I imagine they may be hungry."

"Daughters?" A woman behind her gasped. Rebecca turned and found that it was the woman of the house, Naomi. "You are not married!" Rebecca saw other women turn to glance in their direction, not ashamed to show the disbelief on their faces.

"I apologize for misleading you, Naomi," Rebecca looked around the room suddenly feeling as if the walls were closing in on her. She was trying to explain herself, but the right words were failing her.

Emma stepped up next to her, "She is a widow," she offered, "She did not want to expose herself as he was just recently buried."

Naomi took a step back and placed her hand on her heart, "Oh, my dear. I am so sorry I assumed—I always chastise myself for doing that! I hope that you and your family find peace as this is all just a part of the Lord's plan."

"I know," Rebecca responded, finding her voice again, "We are doing well and trying to move forward with things." The women around her nodded in agreement and each one offered a supportive smile.

"We will pray for you," Naomi added before turning back to her friends.

"Well, as I said, I should be getting back now." Emma took Rebecca's hand and led her outside where they called to Eli.

"I must be going, Eli. I want to thank you for your generosity today, it is most appreciated." Eli smiled and then went into the barn to retrieve her horse. To Rebecca's surprise, it was Jacob who walked out with the horse instead.

"I believe this is yours," Jacob said, grinning.

"Yes," Rebecca reached for the straps, but Jacob held them a moment longer.

"You should come here again."

"Oh? Why is that?"

"I would like to invite you on a walk. I would have asked now, but I know that you have to leave," he explained, "I want to get to know you better." Rebecca was unsure how to respond to this, it appeared as if she met him for a reason and she knew that never before had a man inspired these feelings, not even Tom. *Especially not Tom,* she thought. But how would she explain herself to this man? What would the other women think as they all knew the truth about her situation?

She stopped for a moment and recalled the words from the sermon earlier in the day, *whether we understand—rather, whether we choose to try to understand, this is where we fail.* She did not understand what was happening or why, but she trusted that her response was the right one.

"I would love to."

Chapter 4: The Rendezvous

As she laid down that night, her mind was racing with thoughts of Jacob. She imagined them walking along the river and talking about everything. She knew that she would not be able to hide the truth from him about Tom and her daughters, but she did not want to. She wanted him to know her as she truly was, nothing more and nothing less. She did not know how he would respond, but again, she trusted that they had met for a reason.

She closed her eyes as she dared to imagine him holding her hand as they sat in the grass, staring out into the water. She drifted off to sleep with the sweet beginnings of a dream in her mind.

The next few days went by without anything remarkable and she was grateful for the routine of it all. They woke up and tended to their chores, the afternoons were typically filled with prayers and meeting with friends in the community. She didn't allow herself to think too much of the impending reunion with Jacob for fear that he would not accept her. *He could already know the truth*, Rebecca thought to herself, *all the women know. Emma knows, she may have said something to him.* She forced the thought to the back of her mind before she let it affect her anymore.

The day came and she was preparing the buggy when Sarah walked up to her, "Mama, where are you going?"

"I am going to the community down the way, Sarah," Rebecca looked at her daughter, "I told you and Ruby this last night over supper. Do you not remember?"

"Oh," she looked down at her feet and quietly admitted, "I had forgotten."

"It's alright, Sarah. Sometimes we forget things if we weren't really listening."

Sarah looked up at her mom and asked, "Can I go too, mama?"

"I thought you were playing with your sister?"

"They do not want to play with me today," she said with a disappointed look. Rebecca turned to face her daughter and for the first time in a while, she recognized just how young she truly was. She had her entire life ahead of her.

"Well," said Rebecca taking Sarah into a tight embrace, "I bet if you start playing a fun game, they will ask to play with *you* instead!" Sarah looked at her mother with a big smile and skipped off into the distance, no doubt to find Ruby and her other friends. Rebecca finished preparing the buggy and climbed aboard ready to face Jacob for the first time since the service.

The ride to the community felt longer than the last time and Rebecca hadn't even thought about what she would say to him when she saw him or how she would start the conversation. She quickly realized that she had no idea which house was his or where she might be able to tie up her buggy. Gripped with panic, she was tempted to turn around. *This is too soon*, she told herself, *I am not supposed to be here.*

Just as the thought came to her, she saw him standing there in the middle of the entrance to the community. She smiled to herself and slowed down in order to speak to him.

"Hello, Rebecca."

"Jacob," she nodded towards him trying to rid the smile from her lips and failing.

"You can follow me, I will show you where to park the buggy." She followed closely behind him and he led her to a small barn behind a house. The door to the house swung open and Emma came running outside.

"Rebecca!" she called out. The two women embraced as if they had been friends for years. They laughed together while Jacob took the horse to the stable. "Jacob told me that you would be coming back today. At first, I was confused because there is no service, but then I realized what he was talking about!" she quickly added, "But don't worry, I don't think anyone else knows but me. It's our little secret!" Emma let out a girlish giggle and for the first time, Rebecca realized that Emma must have been at least five or so years younger than herself. She smiled at the girl as Jacob walked towards them both.

"Do I even want to know what you two are talking about already?" Jacob asked playfully.

"Shh," Emma laughed, "He's here!" The two women laughed as Jacob shook his head, but the smile never left his face.

"I thought maybe we could talk a walk by the river," Jacob offered. Rebecca nodded and looked back at Emma who was waving from the stoop.

They walked quietly next to each other for a few minutes before Jacob said, "My sister is quite fond of you."

"Well, from what you have told me, she can be quite fond of everyone."

"This is true," he smiled. Rebecca took a moment to admire his smile—it wasn't perfect, his teeth were not lined up neatly in a row and they did not necessarily sparkle, but his smile was so genuine, it lit up his entire face, and it made the recipient want to smile as well.

"How old is she?" Rebecca asked, "If you don't mind my asking that question."

"Of course not. Emma is now seventeen years old. She is my youngest sister. I have another sister, Mary who is nineteen. I am above her at twenty-two. And then my eldest two sisters, Lorna and Lucinda, they are twins and they are twenty-five. Lorna and Lucinda are both married and live in this community as well."

"Wow, what a blessing to have such a large family. And to be the only boy, that must be fun!" Rebecca joked.

"I like to think I am the greatest body guard that ever lived," he laughed, "Except for the fact that nothing has ever happened to them, so it's been a pretty mundane job." He looked at Rebecca and asked, "So, how about you? Do you have any brothers or sisters?"

"No, I'm afraid. It is just me," Rebecca looked out towards the water as she thought about her life as a child and how lonely she had always been with no siblings to play with. She thought of her own daughter, Sarah, from today and decided that it would be now or never. "I do have two daughters, Sarah and Ruby."

"Yes, Emma told me about them," Jacob said. Rebecca stopped walking suddenly and Jacob turned to face her, "What is it?"

"She told you?"

"Yes, I asked her why you needed to leave from the service and she told me that you had to get home to your daughters."

"Did she tell you anything else?"

"No, that was all. Was that wrong of her to share that information? I'm sorry if that upset you in any way..." he trailed off.

"It isn't that," she sighed, "I just, I didn't know that you knew that and I didn't want to think poorly of me."

"Why would I think poorly of you?"

"My husband, Tom. He recently passed and now it is just the three of us. I did not want you to think—"

"Rebecca," Jacob cut her off mid-sentence and she looked up at him with tears in her eyes. *How foolish*, she thought, *I am crying before a man I hardly know.* "Rebecca, I do not want you to take this in the wrong way at all, but I deeply believe in the power of God's will and I know that He has a plan for all of us. What has happened in your life was just Him making room for what is to come next. We cannot expect you to be grateful to Him for what He has done while also living in the past, unable to move on from it. Here," Jacob held out his hand to her, "take my hand and with every step we take, we move further away from what has happened and move closer to the rest of life's possibilities."

Rebecca looked at his outstretched hand and hesitated for a moment before finally deciding to place her hand in his. He smiled at her and they walked along the edge of the river talking about their families and their lives. Rebecca told him about Tom—both the happy and the not-so-happy times. They walked until the sun started to dip below the horizon.

"I should be going," Rebecca said to Jacob, finally releasing his hand. He nodded and walked her back to the barn where he went inside to retrieve the horse. Emma came running outside of the door as if she had been waiting for their return.

"You must stay for dinner!" she announced.

"I cannot today, Emma. I am sorry. I have to get back to my girls."

"Oh right, of course. Well the next time you come, you must bring them with you!"

"The next time?" Rebecca laughed.

"He did ask you to come back again, didn't he?" Emma looked around for her brother, "Jacob! You didn't ask her to come back again?" she said in utter disbelief.

Jacob laughed at his youngest sister, "I was getting there, Emma."

"Oh," Emma said and her cheeks flushed, "I'm just going to go back inside now." She gave Rebecca a quick hug and ran inside of the house.

"Would you like to come back soon?" He looked so hopeful and Rebecca thought back on the afternoon they spent together. She felt at peace and it was so easy to talk to him about everything.

"I was thinking," Rebecca said quietly, "perhaps you could come to my community. I'd like for you to meet my girls." Jacob beamed at her and nodded in agreement. He helped her onto her buggy and when Rebecca looked back to give him a final wave goodbye, she saw that his eyes had never left her.

Chapter 5: The Meeting

The next day Rebecca and the girls spent the entire day cleaning the house from top to bottom, ensuring that everything was for Jacob's arrival. Rebecca's mother and father came in the afternoon while the girls were busy getting ready.

"I see you are having no trouble keeping things in order," her mother commented. "I don't think I have ever seen the house so clean."

"We are expecting a guest from a different community in a short while," Rebecca explained, slightly off put by her mother's comment.

"Who is coming?" her father asked.

Rebecca looked at the man who sat across from her and took in his sturdy frame built from years of arduous work. Little pieces of grey hair had just started speckling his beard and hair, the only indication of his age. She loved her father dearly and she knew that he wanted his only daughter to be happy.

"Jacob," she replied, "I met him at a service last week." Her mother glanced at her father and waited for his reaction.

"You've invited a man to your home? Rebecca, I do not like this at all," her father pulled at his beard as he always did when something made him uncomfortable.

"Father, I wanted him to meet the girls. And I thought it would be better for all of us if he could meet them where they are most comfortable, in their own home."

"Meet the girls?" her mother exclaimed, "Have you thought about what you are doing? What if others see a man walking into your home knowing that your husband is no longer here?"

"Mother, how can I move forward and truly accept God's plan if people expect me to constantly live in the past?" Her father nodded slowly and folded his hands on top of one another.

"We would like to meet him," he said finally. Neither Rebecca nor her mother thought it wise to go against him so they quietly gave in to him. The girls emerged from their rooms looking as beautiful as ever and ran into their grandparent's arms giving them tight hugs.

The five of them talked amongst themselves until they heard a small knock at the door. Her father stood up and walked over to the wooden entrance, pulling open the door. Jacob reached out his hand immediately and introduced himself. Rebecca's father invited him inside of the house and they all sat and talked about the girls and the communities. They talked about their faith and Rebecca could tell that both her mother and her father were impressed by the strength of Jacob's character.

He is a good man, Rebecca thought to herself, *perhaps I needed to know what life was like before him so that I could truly appreciate the goodness within him.*

Rebecca looked around the room admiring the feeling of warmth and love, a feeling that she had strived for a long time to achieve. Perhaps she didn't fully understand why things happened as they did, but she did know one thing. Whatever God's plan for her, Jacob was certainly a part of it.

GOING HOME

JENNIFER MCDONALD

Rebecca stared at the house. Her eyes didn't see the neat gardens or the paint that had obviously been applied recently, and which kept the house looking tidy. They didn't see the obvious work that the people within, her parents and siblings, had done on it to keep it nice.

All her eyes saw was the fire, the smoke, the broken remnants of the car that had taken her Eli from her.

When she'd talked to him about coming home, it had always been assumed that they would go together. That when they got here, it would be to announce their marriage, and that their families would have to just accept it. They had saved enough money to set up their own house, and that was what she had always assumed would happen.

Now here she was. Crawling back to her parents. Alone and scared and without Eli's comforting presence at her side. She was going to have to face her mother and father for the first time since she'd walked out two years ago.

The plan had been simple, back then. While Rebecca's parents had approved of the potential marriage between her and Eli, Eli's parents had not. They had a different girl in mind for him, and while it was his choice, the pressure they'd put on him to accept their choice had been overwhelming.

So why not leave? Go into the wider world, the one that both of them had only just barely glimpsed during their Rumspringa, and make it on their own? Have some fun, away from the restrictions that his parents, in particular, wanted to put on them?

They'd been eighteen then. It had been two years since then. They'd made the money, working two jobs each. Neither of them had ever been afraid of hard work.

When it came down to it, though, neither of them had ever been comfortable, really, with living together, with living in sin. When they'd both admitted to that, everything had seemingly fallen into place.

They would go home. They would get married before they did so that no one could tear them apart, and then they would raise their kids away from the big city. Philadelphia, they'd both agreed, was no place to raise children. It would be too expensive, and far, far too immoral.

Then came the night that Eli had come to pick her up from work. He'd always been a gentleman like that. He'd learned to drive while in the big city, though, and she hadn't, so even though he was exhausted from his own job, he'd gotten into his cheap, secondhand car and drove through the bad part of town to come get her.

Neither of them had seen the drunk driver coming. Rebecca had been thrown free. She'd walked away from the horrific accident with nothing more than a few bruises, but Eli ...

Blinking back tears, Rebecca straightened her shoulders and forced her eyes to come back into focus. She had to see what was in front of her. She was alone, and she would continue to be alone unless she could get her parents to agree to take her back.

Maybe she could have kept living in the city, but the rent there was so expensive, especially for one person. Besides, without Eli, it didn't feel quite right. Nothing did. Going back home was the only option that she had, and part of her, quite a large part, yearned for it.

Life had been exciting in Philadelphia, but it had also been complicated. Complex. Life with her parents had always been simple, and she craved that simplicity now just as much as she had rebelled against it two years ago.

She'd thrown away most of her Amish clothing when she'd left for the big city, but thankfully, she'd kept one dress and her white bonnet. When she looked down at herself, she looked much as she had on that fateful day when she and Eli, full of hopes and dreams, had walked away and hadn't looked back. Not until years later, anyway.

She just hoped that it wasn't too late.

Taking a deep, deep breath, she let it out slowly, forcing the tears from her eyes. Philadelphia didn't feel like home, but neither did her parents' house. Was there anywhere on the planet for her anymore? Or had she, with her recklessness, lost that forever?

How long she would have stood there, just staring, she didn't know. But she heard the familiar squeaks, the heavy clip-clop of horse's feet, and moved out of the way of the buggy that she knew was coming without having to give any thought to it at all.

As she moved, she looked to see who was driving the buggy. The man she saw there was no different from many of the other men in their settlement, at least on the surface. He was bearded, dressed all in black, a hat perched atop his head. It had been strange, in the big city, seeing people who didn't wear hats most of the time ...

And then her eyes met the man's, and she flinched away. Eli's brother, Samuel, looked back at her, just for a second, his eyes burning into hers. There could be no doubt that he recognized her.

The buggy rolled on, and Rebecca drew one deep, shuddering breath into her lungs, which had been starved of oxygen through the entire encounter. Samuel, who would doubtless go tell his father and mother, who had never much cared for Rebecca and surely now despised her, would soon know that she was back.

That thought provided her the impetus that she needed. It was enough to have her walking around the yard and up the stairs, her sensible black shoes muffled as she went to the door and knocked on it firmly.

It was her mother who answered the door. Her mother, who looked just the same as she always had, with her kind, dark eyes. Her mother, and until Rebecca laid eyes on her again, she hadn't realized just how much she actually missed this woman.

She hadn't meant to cry, she really hadn't. She'd been pushing tears back ever since the accident that had taken Eli away from her. Strange to think that it had only been a week ago. It felt like it had been a lifetime since he'd last touched her.

When her mother opened her arms to Rebecca without a word, that was all it took to rip down that wall that she'd put up around her heart. The wall that had let her do what it was necessary for her to do, which had held back all of her emotions and let her put her affairs in order so that she could make her way home.

Home. Home was in her mother's arms, crying on her shoulder. Home was the rest of the family, her three brothers, and her baby sister, coming out to greet her, to wrap her up in family affection that did a fair bit to salve the pain inside her.

Family was where, when you had to go there, they had to take you in. She'd heard it said as a joke, but in that moment, she knew that it was also nothing but the truth.

* * *

"Rebecca King, I need to speak with you," Miriam, her mother, said firmly. It was a week after Rebecca had come home, and she knew that she hadn't been very useful in that time. She had helped her mother around the house, with the cooking and the cleaning, a little bit, but that was it.

It was unlike her, and her mother, who knew her better than most people did, would know that.

Rebecca closed her eyes briefly, trying to brace herself for what was going to come next. Demands about what she'd done while she was in the city, perhaps. Questions about Eli, though Rebecca knew that their community had received news about Eli's death. She knew because she'd been the one to send it to his parents. They would have gotten the letter she'd sent the day after the accident.

She couldn't handle being grilled about it. Her own loss was still far too fresh. Still, she was mindful of the Fifth Commandment, and she figured that she hadn't done an amazing job of honoring her father or her mother so far. She owed it to the woman to at least try.

"What are you planning to do with your life now?" the woman asked, which wasn't at all the way that Rebecca had expected this conversation to go. "Are you going to just stay in your bed and mope forever?"

Rebecca closed her eyes and winced a little. Her mother didn't mean to be unkind. In fact, 'unkind' was pretty much the last word that could be applied to Miriam King. She was, however, matter of fact, pragmatic, and not one to hold back from speaking her mind.

"I know you've lost someone important to you, my child," Miriam said, her tone more gentle. "And I grieve with you. Eli would have made a fine son-in-law. But God has called him home, and you're still here. You're still alive."

Those words sparked something in Rebecca, something that she hadn't felt in quite some time. After a moment, she recognized it as hope. It wasn't a bright, shining hope, like when she'd left with Eli, but it was the hope that maybe her life didn't have to be over.

"I'll help you more," Rebecca promised. She knew that Miriam worked hard, and felt briefly ashamed for her own sadness, which she'd allowed to make her idle. Instead, she would channel it into hard work. "Cleaning, sewing, cooking ... I remember how to do it."

"Do you think," Miriam asked, after a long silence, "That you'll get married?" Her voice was gentle but it still made Rebecca ache inside in a way that she wasn't sure she would ever fully recover from. That wound would never fully heal.

The question was innocuous enough, but they both knew what Miriam was asking. How serious had the relationship been? That wasn't something that Rebecca was willing to discuss with her conservative mother, though.

"Do I have to decide that right now?" Rebecca asked, and her mother reached over and gave her a hug, just a brief one, but one that meant the world to Rebecca. Her mother loved her, that she knew. That meant something, especially since Rebecca knew that she'd put her through a lot.

"No, of course not," Miriam said, and Rebecca nodded. After a brief pause during which she struggled with herself, she gave a soft sigh.

It was the right thing to do, even if it wasn't exactly easy for her to do it. Still, she could humble herself, if she had to, and in this case, she did.

"I'm sorry, mother," she said quietly. "I'm sorry for leaving without telling you."

Her words surprised the older woman, she could tell that, but after a long, silent, awkward moment, her mother replied to her.

"And I'm sorry that I didn't fight harder for you and Eli. I always just thought that it was your choice, your decision, but maybe if I'd spoken to his parents ..."

Through the years, Rebecca had had the same thoughts, and hearing them said aloud was comforting. She smiled and hugged her mother again, and with that, she started to move on with her life.

She would never, never forget Eli, she knew that. He would be in her heart forever. But her mother was right. She was still alive, she had her whole life ahead of her, and it was time to start living that life.

It seemed the perfect way to honor Eli's memory, to stay alive and vibrant, just as he had always been.

* * *

For a couple of weeks, it was enough to just stay in the house. She kept remembering the way that Eli's brother had looked at her, and it seemed to her that it was going to be much safer for her to stay away from the general community. The last thing that she wanted was to cause a scene with Eli's family.

Her world, however, had been expanded by her life in the city. At the time, it had been scary, but it had changed her. The walls of her parents' house started to seem more and more restrictive, and eventually, she felt like they were closing in on her.

She wasn't going to be able to sit around in the house all day, sewing and cleaning. She knew what it was like to go out and do something for a living. Her jobs had never been anything special, but she'd felt needed, valued.

The answer to her solution came home with her father one day. He'd been helping one of the other men paint his house, and he walked into the house with big news on his lips.

"Rachel Fisher is getting married."

That was a big deal. Rachel Fisher had been the one and only teacher for many years. Rebecca herself had been instructed in the one room schoolhouse for a couple of years.

Rachel must have been pushing thirty, which was quite the age for a woman to be unmarried, at least in their community. Once she was married, she wouldn't be able to teach. She'd be expected to go take care of her own new family.

All of a sudden, she had it. She knew what she was supposed to be doing, as clear as day. It was almost like someone had spoken the words to her. Like someone had directed her to what she was meant to be doing.

"I will apply for that job."

The sense of rightness only intensified as she said the words. Yes. This was what she was meant to be doing. Even the look that her parents exchanged didn't deflate that sense of purpose in the slightest.

"Rebecca ... That may be difficult, given your past," her father said, his tone doubtful. Rebecca frowned, but listened, leaning forward, the sock that she was darning lying forgotten in her lap.

"I feel like it's what I'm meant to do," Rebecca said. "Yes, I left, but I was called back, don't you see? I can teach the children."

Her father nodded slowly. He was a man of a deep Godliness, and she could tell that her own conviction was swaying him.

"There's a problem, my daughter," Rebecca's mother said, and Rebecca turned to look at her, one eyebrow arched in wordless question. "Amos Fisher."

Instantly, Rebecca understood. The teachers were hired by a committee of three local men, local parents, influential in the community. Somehow, she'd always known that Amos was one of them, but it had never occurred to her to think about what that meant for her before.

Amos Fisher, Rachel's father. Rachel, who was Eli's older sister.

In short, if Rebecca wanted the job, she was going to have to convince a man who hated her that she deserved it.

* * *

Her chance came sooner than she would have imagined.

Rebecca knew that no one thought that she had a chance. Even her own parents, who had been supportive, were sure that she would be frozen out. That there was no chance that Amos would hire her, given his opinion of her.

However, she knew that her own father had told Amos and the other two men that she was interested. Not that she had a lot of hope for that, although she was the most experienced woman who was unmarried. There were very few women of the right age, who had finished school themselves, and of those few, who knew how many were interested?

So when Rebecca went to the dry goods store to get some more cloth for the sewing needs of her family, she was secretly elated to see that Amos was there, too, browsing through some farming implements. This was exactly the sort of meeting that she'd been dreading only a short time ago. Now, however, she couldn't have felt more eager for it.

This was her future that she was fighting for, she reminded herself. Not just because of her wish to be a teacher, but just in general. If she wanted to be accepted, truly accepted, then she was going to have to neutralize Amos.

So, feeling bold, she approached him. It was not something that most of the Amish women would have done, and her insides felt like they were all a-quiver with nerves, but it was necessary.

"Good afternoon," Rebecca said, keeping her voice quiet, but speaking directly to Amos. She kept looking at him, even when it seemed that his first reaction was to simply ignore her, and eventually, he nodded briefly at her, his expression blank.

It wasn't much, but she took it as an encouraging sign.

"I was wondering if you had had a chance to decide who you wish to hire as the new teacher," Rebecca continued, though Amos hardly seemed to be in a talkative mood. Still, it was a fair question, not one that very many people could take offense to.

He, apparently, was an exception to the general rule.

"Not a whore who took my son from me, who got him killed," Amos said, and while Rebecca had tried to keep her voice down, Amos was doing no such thing. He spoke as though inviting the few other patrons of the store to listen to him, to watch as he shamed her. "Not someone who abandoned her people. Why would I bring a viper into a place where children are supposed to learn?"

Rebecca flinched back from him. She wasn't used to being spoken to that way, and a deep, intense, enervating shame filled her. His words were harsh, but were they fair? Hadn't she been the one to get Eli killed?

"You should have stayed in the city," Amos said, and Rebecca felt the blood rush to her cheeks. Suddenly, she felt dizzy, nauseated. "You should have stayed where you belonged, and never darkened the doorsteps of anyone that you betrayed again."

With that, he left, and Rebecca fell back against a display, which was luckily made of strong wood and could support her. Right there, in front of at least ten people, she threw up, closing her eyes against the vertigo and the weakness that threatened to claim her completely.

She had to be helped home by the kind, compassionate daughter of the man who ran the dry goods store.

* * *

Within the next few days, two important things happened.

The first was that Amos and the other men agreed on a teacher to hire, and it wasn't Rebecca. After her run in with the man in the store, she could hardly be surprised by that. She had seen it coming, in all honesty.

The second was much more unexpected. It had been over a month that she'd been back, and she realized, after her disgraceful performance in the store, that during that whole time, she hadn't had her monthly courses even once. Not only that, but her breasts ached, her nipples had darkened, and she felt sick almost all of the time.

After a conversation with her mother that she hoped was discreet enough to keep the older woman in the dark, she had to come to the conclusion that she had been avoiding.

She was with child. With Eli's child. She, an unmarried woman, possibly on her own very soon if her parents decided to kick her out, was going to have a baby.

* * *

The question of how she was going to tell her parents plagued her. She started sleeping more, just as she had when she'd first arrived here, claiming that she had an illness that sapped all of her strength.

It wasn't like that was even inaccurate.

It even occurred to her, as she emptied her stomach once more, holding her hair back from her face, that she could just let nature take its toll. In a few short months, her condition would be obvious to anyone who looked at her. Then she wouldn't have to tell anyone at all.

That's when her mother came in, and when she saw Rebecca crouched down, the older woman sighed and took over the job of holding her hair back.

"How long have you known?" she asked Rebecca, who just shook her head, utterly miserable. Without a word, her mother knew. Of course, she did. Rebecca had hoped otherwise, but it didn't actually surprise her. The woman had been pregnant many times herself, it made perfect sense that she would see the symptoms and recognize them.

"I'm sorry," Rebecca whispered, and she was. All she'd done, it seemed, was bring shame to her family, and she hated that. All she'd wanted to do was follow her heart, but she'd made a mess of all of it.

She had no life ahead of her, and they both knew that without needing to be told. No future at all. She was pregnant, out of wedlock, and she couldn't even marry the father.

"Why did you do it? I thought we taught you better than that." Rebecca's mother's voice was more sad and disappointed than angry, and that, somehow, was far worse.

"It was just once. We were going to get married before we came back," Rebecca said, and then buried her face in her hands and burst into hopeless tears.

It had been bad enough when she'd just been the one who had left and come back. Now she was going to be raising a baby, all on her own. Her parents might even be shunned, utterly ostracized, and she almost certainly would be.

"I wish I'd just stayed, mother," Rebecca said, as she felt her mother's warm, comforting arms wrapping around her, hugging her close. "I wish that I'd married Eli here. That I'd been willing to wait long enough to get his parents' blessing."

Her voice died down, and then, after a long moment, she whispered,

"Maybe then Eli would still be alive."

"Listen to me, Rebecca," her mother said, her tone stern, the voice that Rebecca had always known meant that she was in trouble, that she was being chastised. "I can tell that you think it was your fault. It wasn't. You didn't cause Eli's death."

Rebecca squeezed her eyes against the tears that kept coming, no matter how hard she tried to restrict them. She shook her head. They hadn't even spoken about this, and she was utterly touched by her mother's faith.

Touched, and then even more ashamed, because she was going to have to let her down once more.

"I loved him," Rebecca sobbed, "But I got him killed. He was picking me up from work, mother. He was tired from working his two jobs, but he came to get me so that I could be safe. It was my fault."

Her mother shook her head, her hands warm and comforting on Rebecca's back.

"No, my daughter. That wasn't your fault. Eli did the right thing. It was the fault of the one who caused the accident. I know Eli well enough to know that it couldn't have been him."

Rebecca shook her head. Eli had been driving carefully, as he always did.

"The car ... it came out of nowhere," Rebecca whispered. It hurt to say the words. It hurt to think about it at all. But maybe it was the good kind of hurt, the kind where she was getting rid of something that was festering deep in her soul.

"Any part you had in it, God forgives you, if you repent," Rebecca heard her mother whisper, and the words helped. For the first time, she thought that maybe, just maybe, she could eventually get over what had happened.

With the help of her family, of course, and her Heavenly Father.

* * *

Perhaps it should have tempted her more than it did to go back to the big city. There, no one would even think twice about the fact that she was a single woman with a baby. Sure, there was some stigma around it, but from what she'd seen, it was so common that there was a really good chance that no one would pay much attention.

Besides, she had someone else that she had to think about now. The baby that was, day by day, growing inside her, developing and forming and getting ready to be born. A baby, who was depending on her, above all else.

No. She and Eli had talked about this a great deal. They had never wanted to raise their children in the city. They'd wanted their children to be raised in their faith, in safety, without the bad influences of the city life to impact them.

The temptation wasn't there, not really. Yes, if she left, she wouldn't have to deal with being shamed for what she'd done, what she and Eli had done, but at the same time, there would be so many other problems.

Anyway, it was her actions, and she needed to take responsibility for them. Running away had been a bit of a bad habit for her, and it was a habit that it was time to break.

Even knowing that, however, it took her a good few months to get herself ready for what she knew that she needed to do. Amos Fisher was the grandfather of this child, and he needed to know that she was carrying his son's baby. There was really no other option.

It was terrifying, though. Each and every time she thought about doing it, she felt a deep, painful shame burning in the pit of her very being. She remembered staggering into the wooden display, she remembered the painful bite of it into her lower back, the horrific sensation of everyone looking at her.

Once more, she found herself confined to the house. That suited her just fine, actually. There was always work to do, and slowly, her skill at doing it came back to her.

Along with a surprising sense of satisfaction in the simple tasks. As a child, she'd hated sewing, and cooking, and chafed under the restrictions. As an adult, however, she could lose herself in the rhythms of sewing, and take pride in what she'd made with her own hands, in the satisfaction of feeding her family, in helping.

There was a lot of wisdom to this way of life. It made a lot of sense, and when she was away from the distractions of the city, she found that she had more time to sit back and to just think. To be with herself, to value her interactions with her family.

It was too bad that she would probably be driven out of the community completely once everyone knew that she was pregnant and that she wasn't married to the father.

Day by day, her body changed. At first, it was slow, in almost invisible ways. No one would have noticed, not other than herself. But as the weeks moved on, her stomach, which had been flat and taut, started to gradually round, and she knew that she was running out of time.

Her parents were the only ones that knew. That had been fine when the whole thing had been easily hidden, but what was she supposed to do now that her body was changing? Yes, she could stay hidden in the house, but her family often had visitors, being well respected in the community.

She couldn't hide it forever.

If nothing else, in about five more months, she would have a baby. That would be hard to hide. Not only that, but she wouldn't want her child to have to hide. What sort of life would that be for him or for her? She'd wanted the baby to be raised with the same sort of love and community that she had always felt here.

Besides, she was going to have to carve out some sort of place for her child. There weren't exactly very many children wandering around in this area without both a mother and a father.

It was actually sort of an unknown for her. How people would react, how they would treat her, yes, but also, how they would treat her child, who was blameless in all of this. She just didn't know, and that was utterly terrifying, that made her stomach clench and her heart pound sickeningly.

Still, she knew what she needed to do. In a few short months, her baby would be born, and she had to do her best to make sure there would be a place for them here. Which meant that, as tempting as it was to run or hide, she couldn't do it.

Even knowing that, however, it took a fair bit of time for her to actually come around to doing what needed to be done. Each day, she woke up, determined that that day would be the day. Each day, she ended up deciding that the next day would be better, for one reason or another, none of them entirely made up but neither were they exactly genuine.

It was only when she reached down one morning and felt the gentle curve of her stomach as it started to swell that she realized that she had run out of time. If she didn't go to see Amos, she was risking that someone else would tell him first. Maybe that would be easier on her, but it also wasn't at all fair.

How was she going to bring it up? She agonized over that as she dressed in the clothing that still fit, though only just barely, and modestly covered her braided hair in a white cap. What were the perfect words to use to make the man, who was, she knew, a genuinely good man, understand? Yes, he was a good man, but he was also inflexible, unyielding, maybe even stubborn.

She still didn't know when she left the house, but it didn't matter. Today really was the day, and if she had to make it up as she went along, so be it.

* * *

It was a long walk. Rebecca's parents' farm was big, and while the Fisher family farm was only a few farms away, it was still going to take her a couple of hours to walk that distance. Not only was it fairly far, since all of the farms were relatively large, but she wasn't moving all that quickly these days.

Though her energy was coming back, she noticed. The early days of her pregnancy had left her exhausted. She wouldn't be sad to leave that behind.

Still, even after the walk, she arrived at the farm, still having no idea what to say. Which she couldn't let stop her from walking up to the front porch and squaring her shoulders before knocking.

Amos himself, who must have been in for lunch, opened the door. His look of polite inquiry transformed itself into anger immediately, and he opened his mouth, no doubt to say something cutting, to send her away.

She couldn't let that happen.

All of her half-formed plans flew out of her head, and she looked him directly in the eye and ended up just blurting the words out.

"I'm with child. In five months, I will have Eli's baby."

There. It was out. The words that she'd been tormenting herself over how to say, they were out there in the open. It had been her obligation, to Eli and to his family, to say them, and now, she had.

There was a long, long silence, and then Amos nodded. It was impossible for her to know what he was thinking. He'd never been the sort of man to talk about his emotions all that much. The one exception that she could think of was when he'd gotten so angry at the store.

Not a good thing for her to think about.

"Who is it, Amos?" a woman's voice called. A familiar voice. It was Charity Fisher, Eli's mother.

"It's Rebecca King," Amos said, and his voice cracked, just the tiniest bit, on the last syllable. "She's brought us news."

Charity came out, standing beside her husband, looking at Rebecca with curiosity, just faintly tinged with hostility. Charity had never been quite as displeased with Rebecca as Amos had, but doubtless, she wasn't her biggest fan ever since Rebecca had run off with Eli.

Rebecca took a deep breath, and she almost reached out to take Charity's hand. The grandmother of her child, of Eli's child. She wanted to touch her, to form some sort of link, but in the end, she didn't quite dare.

"I'm pregnant," she said softly. "Please, don't ... I just thought that you should know. That you both should know. You're going to be grandparents."

To her surprise, Rebecca saw tears in Charity's eyes. Amos still wasn't saying anything, but Charity, acting apparently on an impulse, reached out and did what Rebecca hadn't quite dared to do. She took Rebecca's hands and squeezed them.

"What wonderful news," Charity said, and her voice was much more emotional. Her fingers, when they grasped Rebecca, were tight and her hands were shaking just a little bit.

Charity missed Eli just as much as Rebecca did, she realized with wonder. This whole time, she'd been living alone with her grief, when there was a woman right here who could have potentially shared that with her.

If only Rebecca had been brave enough to reach out to her, and not just Amos, before.

"We were never married," Rebecca ventured hesitantly. She hated to bring it up, but she didn't want there to be any more lying, any more hiding things or secrets, between them.

Charity nodded.

"It doesn't matter," the older woman said. "As of this day, you are my daughter. I will help you to raise the child, and so, I know, will your mother."

It was unconventional, to be sure, but then, the whole situation was. Maybe it didn't have to be the tragedy that she'd always assumed it would be, however. Maybe, just maybe, things could work out for her.

"I'll need the help," Rebecca said, laughing through the tears in her own eyes, the ones that mirrored Chastity's. "And you have the experience." Chastity had, after all, given birth to a dozen children. She knew what she was doing.

With this woman, she knew that her baby would be safe. She knew that Chastity, once she'd decided that a child was hers, would defend it until the end.

She had no doubt at all that the woman would do the same for her grandchild, as well.

Slowly, Rebecca, still holding Chastity's hands, looked over at Amos, who had yet to say much of anything. Who was standing there, staring at her?

She'd won over Chastity, perhaps. Or the baby had, anyway, which was good enough. What of Amos, though? She watched him, just waiting. Could he unbend enough to allow her into his life, for the sake of his son? For the sake of his son's child?

For a moment, the tension stretched between them, and Rebecca became more and more sure that he would make her leave. That he would hurl cruel words at her, just as he had in the store. He wasn't the sort of man that would normally give up a grudge, not when his anger was righteous.

"God forgive me," Amos said suddenly, and to her surprise, she saw that his eyes were suspiciously shiny, as well, like he might be holding back some emotions of his own. "I drove you away."

"I forgive you if you will do the same for me," Rebecca nodded, and Amos considered that for a long moment before nodding.

"Welcome to the Fisher family, Rebecca," he said, finally saying the words that were all that she'd wanted to hear for so long.

She had a home, and so did her baby.

They would be safe.

The End

THE SHY AMISH BRIDE

NATALIE MEYER

Three best friends, Betty, Amity and Rachel are practically inseparable. But when they land themselves in a stormy predicament on their way home on night a newcomer in town comes to their rescue. All three girls show an interest in the handsome stranger, but only one of them would walk away with the prize. What starts off as nothing but a playful bet between friends, ends up surprising them all.

Uri Guth came to Derby Creek to start afresh, the last thing he expected was to fall in love. But when he meets the shy red head who reminded him autumn, he pulled out all stops. He knew the moment he laid eyes on her that she was his match.

Chapter 1

Rain just kept falling, never ending without any intention to stop, large puddles had gathered on the muddy grounds around the big barn, and water gushed down the eroded embankment running alongside the road, causing the road to be completely flooded. But no amount of rain would prevent Amity, Betty and Rachel to do what they came here to do. Having been friends since childhood, the three women were inseparable. Neither of them were married or promised to anyone yet, and although they are well beyond the age most girls in their community starts to settle down to start a family, it never really bothered them.

Amity was strong willed and mouthy young woman, who voiced her opinion whenever she felt it mattered. Of course her father, Bishop Gunther didn't quite approve of her behaviour at times, but he did support her willingness to stand up for herself. Bishop Gunther on the other hand wasn't like most others in their faith; he was more lenient and accepting than most, always promoting change within reason. He insisted that households started using gas stoves instead of coal stoves. He had even arranged to buy a truck to help the community to cart goods to the local market in town. According to him, modern change to a bare minimum does not give the devil a foothold, it just shows the devil that they are capable of change without modern ways ruling their lives and changing who they are or distracting them from things that matter most.

Betty, much like Amity also had a strong personality, one she definitely got from her mother, but she also had a mischievous streak. When the elders instructed the children not to play in the rain, she was always the first to splash in muddy puddles. When they had their social events, she was the one who would pull pranks, like stuff a mouse in someone's pocket or stick a dish to a table cloth with workman's glue, causing a huge disaster when someone tries to pick it up. All innocent pranks at most, but that was how everyone knew her and more often than not, when she was younger her father would ground her for punishment, but she always found a way out of it.

And then there was Rachel, shy quiet Rachel. More like the runt of the litter, she was one of few words and always just tagged along because Amity and Betty insisted. Rachel only had a father; her mother died giving birth to her. Her father eventually married Elsa, a widow with two sons, who she never got on with. They were two brats and she ended up spending more time with her friends than her own family and over the years, the trio had become the best of friends

Betty giggled and Amity squirmed on the bale of hay, "I bet you David looks like that when he takes his shirt off," she said pointing to the male model in the fashion magazine.

Amity giggled, "It's scandalous! If your dad knew you had these, he'll shun us all," she said in jest.

Rachel, curious as ever, was sitting on the left, also peeking at the magazine, one of the few they kept hidden in the barn under one of the wooden floor slats. They always snuck to the barn to page through the magazines and weigh every other man in their town up against the likes of models that posed so shamelessly with nothing but pair of underpants on.

"*Jah!* Well he doesn't know now does he?" Betty said and paged through a few more pages.

Rachel would never admit it out rightly but she also felt a slight tingle of excitement when she looked at these magazines, they were not overly crude, but they showed more flesh than she had ever seen in her life. Maybe it was because of this, that they were all still single, she thought. Comparing the local boys to those men were like comparing apples with onions.

A sudden noise quickly alerted them and Betty shoved the magazine behind the bale of hay they were seated on. Both Amity and Betty grabbed their egg baskets, while Rachel stood around looking as guilty as ever.

"Betty, are you girls here?"

It was Betty's father who called, and Rachel's stomach lurched, if the Bishop had any idea what they were up to they will be in so much trouble.

"We're here *daed*!" Betty called and dusted the hay off of her dress, "We were caught in the rain, and was waiting for it to pass," she said as her Bishop Gunther appeared.

"I thought so, well I have come to get you girls home, the storm is a long way from being over," he said and handed each of them a rain coat, "Better we hurry, or the storm will catch up with us," he urged them as he let each one of the girls walk towards the barn door ahead of him.

The sky was dark and it wasn't just a summer shower, it was a downpour that looked more like a waterfall from heaven. Heavy drops struck the ground tunnelling into the earth. Up ahead stood the buggy, which didn't offer much or any shelter and Rachel wasn't so sure if they would make it to their respective homes in one piece. Betty was the first to step into the rain, followed by Amity. Bishop Gunther looked at her and nodded, and then in a huddled group the four of them ran towards the buggy, careful not to slip and fall.

Thankful that there was still some daylight to guide the way, the three girls clung to each other as Betty's father steered the buggy towards the house. Hardly able to see a few feet ahead of them and on a treacherous road that has been washed away in most places, Bishop Gunther was still able to make them feel at ease. He didn't even look worried, but then again, that was probably how a man of God should be, like Paul walking on water.

The buggy wheels rattled as they rode over rocks and muddy trenches formed by the mass of water running diagonally across the small road. And a trip that normally took less than fifteen minutes to travel, now seemed like an eternity. They were slowly making their way ahead through the stormy downpour, unbeknownst to Bishop Gunther, the road up ahead had turned into complete sludge and the moment the buggy reached it, the wheels simply slid into a deep trench on the side of the road, pulling the buggy, with the horse off and on to the side of the road. The girls screamed in panic as the buggy slowly leaned over to its side, threatening to topple over. Rachel was the first to clobber out and then helped the other two on to the road. Betty got out safely, but as Amity stumbled out of the buggy, she stepped in a hole and twisted her ankle.

"Ow!!" she cried out as she fell to the ground grabbing for her ankle.

"Amity!" Betty cried and ducked down to help her friend, "Where does it hurt?"

Bishop Gunther also hunched down and looked at her ankle, "It's quite swollen, I think you may have sprained it, can you try and step on it?"

Betty and her father helped Amity to her feet, but the moment she put weight on her injury, she cried out in agony.

"We will have to get you home, just lean on me and Betty" the Bishop said. He studied the state of the buggy, "The buggy will have to stay here until morning."

"But papa, we can hardly see in front of us," Betty lamented as she supported her friend.

"The Lord will light our way," Rachel said confidently and gave Betty a gentle reassuring squeeze.

With Amity supported by Bishop Gunther and Betty, and Rachel next to them carrying the egg baskets, they started down the path taking carful steps in the dark.

Through the stormy gale and rain that kept showering, they heard a galloping sound that sounded more like thunder coming towards them and the next moment, a man on horseback arrived completely drenched.

Rachel couldn't make out his face, but right now he was the best thing that could have happened to them.

"Bishop, Maryanne sent me to see what was keeping you," he shouted over the raging storm, "What happened to the buggy?"

Rachel took over from the Bishop, while he explained to the stranger exactly what had happened, and suggested that they come to recover the buggy in the morning once the rain has passed.

"Betty, you will have to get on the horse with Amity, Rachel you will walk with Uri and I," the Bishop instructed and then the stranger named Uri, helped Amity, and then Betty on to the horse.

Together they slowly made their way back to society, the first stop was Amity's house, where the Bishop helped to get her inside, and seen to, then it was Rachel's turn and finally Uri, Bishop Gunther and Betty made their way to the Bishop's house.

~*~

After Rachel had changed into her night dress and towel dried her wet hair, she deposited herself in front of the fire place. The night had turned out a complete disaster. She was sure it was punishment for their bad behaviour. Lusting like that over fictitious men and so on. She wrapped her quilt around her shoulders and reached for her bible. She knew better than to let her judgement be influenced by anyone. Despite the guilt, she somehow found her mind drifting to the stranger who came to their aid. She still couldn't see his face clearly, but she was sure he was handsome, and strong.

She shook her head to chase away the thoughts and closed her eyes, and said a silent prayer of repentance. She was never going to look at those magazines again.

Chapter 2

The sun broke through the parted curtains in Rachel's room and she pinched her eyes shut. The night before had taken its toll on her, and resulted in her oversleeping when there was still so much to do. She was yet to feed the geese and get ready to go to the local market to deliver the eggs she had collected the day before, but she simply had no will power.

"Rachel!" Her step-mother called from the kitchen, "Come have your breakfast!"

Rachel covered her eyes with her forearm and sighed. She just needed a few more minutes of sleep, but she knew where her priorities lay. She willed herself out of bed and rushed around the room to get ready for the day. By the time she got to the kitchen her mother had already cleaned the dishes, and Rachel's breakfast was waiting.

"The Bishop and his friend were here earlier," Elsa commented in passing, "Looks like you girls had a rough night."

"Yeah, we got caught in the storm," she mumbled.

So the stranger is one of the Bishop's friends, which means he was old, she thought to herself.

"Apparently Amity had twisted her ankle quite badly, but she will be fine in a few days."

"I figured. She stepped in a hole when she tried to get out of the buggy, we couldn't see much."

Elsa came to sit at the table with her, "You girls need to be more careful, things could have been a lot worse."

Sometimes Rachel couldn't help but wonder what Elsa's agenda really was. At times she treated her like a stranger, barely paying attention to her, and other times she came across all motherly. And all this time Rachel had no choice but to keep her own emotions all bottled up.

"We will," Rachel said and stood up to wash her plate, "I'm taking the eggs to the market, is there anything you need me to do?"

"Oh not to worry about the eggs, I've already sold delivered them this morning."

Rachel felt as if she could crush the plate in her hands. Those eggs were her eggs, her income. She was saving money for herself, and now Elsa had taken the little bit she could earn for herself.

"Thank you," she said tight lipped without turning around.

"I hope you don't mind, your father does need some money to buy that new gas stove so, I figured every penny would help."

"Of course," Rachel turned around this time, with a fake smile plastered on her face, "I'll just get more eggs to get money for my new dress."

"Why on earth would you need a new dress?" Elsa said with mock surprise, "Don't you have enough as it is?"

Rachel was slowly starting to lose her temper, but she fought hard to remain calm, "I only have three dresses, and I need one for church, the others are all worn and faded."

Elsa laughed, "It's not like you'll be catching anyone's eye, and you're past the point of marriage. You're already considered a spinster."

"I'm only twenty-two, the same age my mother married," Rachel protested.

"And see how that turned out."

Elsa had barely said the words when her sons, Caleb and Alfred came into the kitchen, and Rachel had to hide her anger. She simply scooped up her empty egg baskets and stormed out of the house. How that woman dared say such heartless things and get away with it, was beyond her she thought as she marched determinedly in no particular direction. But as the anger subsided, it was replaced by doubt. Maybe it was too late for her to marry, but then the same applied to Betty and Amity, they were both the same age. Obviously living in Derby Creek wasn't much help either, there were far more women than men here, and unless they had gatherings from nearby towns, chances of finding a suitor was slim.

First of all there was Betty, who insisted that she was waiting for Mr Right, she refused to settle for less, then there's Amity who also had her own ideas of a suitor, and the few men that did ask for her hand in the past, were coldly turned down because she was just not interested. Rachel always thought that Amity was the kind who would go on a Rumspringa if her father allowed her, out of the three friends, she was the adventurous one.

Rachel grunted a loud oomph as she collided with someone sending her baskets flying. Thankfully they were empty; otherwise they would both have been covered in egg yolk. She stumbled back and started to apologize profusely when she swallowed her words, and a pair of very strong hands cupped her shoulders.

"Are you alight?" the young man asked, and offered her a lopsided smile.

"Jah, I am fine, I-I wasn't paying attention, I'm sorry," she said struggling to breathe.

"It's quite alright, you were miles away there for a second, I'm Uri, Rachel right?" he said and released her as he tucked his thumbs into his suspenders.

Uri, the name immediately rang a bell. He was Bishop Gunther's friend, but how? He was so young, she wondered.

"How do you know my name?" she asked foolishly.

"I came to your rescue last night in the storm, but I suppose you won't recognise me, it was rather dark."

"Oh! Oh right, yes. Well... um, I'll be going now. Thank you, I mean sorry, I... I have to go."

Rachel just about ran away from him, she had acted like a complete and utter fool, stuttering over her words like a second grader having to do an oral assignment. No wonder she was single. She couldn't sit in the company of a man without feeling awkward. As she hurried away she could feel his eyes burn into the back of her, but she refused to glance back. The farther she got away the quicker her out of control heart and raging butterflies would quieten down.

"Rachel!" It was Betty who waved her down, "Where are you heading?"

"Eggs!"

"You're going to Eggs?" Betty giggled.

"No, ugh, I'm going to collect eggs silly," she corrected herself as Betty fell into step next to her, "How is Amity doing?"

"She's fine, but you look like you've seen a ghost, why are you in such a hurry," Betty said as she tried to keep up to Rachel's pace.

"I need to sell enough eggs to buy a new dress. The cow sold all the eggs I collected yesterday."

"What a cow, did she not even ask you?"

"Does she ever?"

The rest of the way, the two friends walked in silence, Betty on her own planet, and Rachel trying to get Uri out of her mind. She hadn't expected him to be so young, nor did she expect him to know her name. The night before was a bit of a blur with everything going on, and she mostly remembered walking beside Bishop Gunther while Uri guided the horse by its reins with Amity and Betty on horseback.

"Is Uri your…"

"Don't you think Uri is…"

They both said at the same time and then burst out laughing.

"Uri is so handsome," Betty continued, "The last time I saw him was when we were kids. His family has been in Germany for the past few years."

"I didn't expect him to be so young," Rachel said, "Are they staying here?"

"Only Uri, he's staying at our house and is helping papa with a few things."

Rachel could hear by Betty's tone that she was keen on Uri, and she knew by the seam of her dress, that Amity will be just as taken by him.

One of them will most certainly catch his eyes, she thought and smiled softly. Her friends or at least one of them deserved a good strong man to care for them.

She dismissed the notion of Uri straight away, knowing that she would never stand a chance. She could hardly string together a proper sentence when she bumped into him earlier.

Chapter 3

Amity humped along with a crutch in one hand, while Betty excitedly skipped besides them. For the first time in who knows how long, Betty and Amity had made some effort to look presentable, both of them had brand new dresses. It was the Friday night frolic, where most boys got to voice their intentions.

Betty was nervous; as usual she was shy and nervous. She never liked these events much, she did not trust the thing called love, her father loved once, he had promised his her mother that he would make sure she was taken care of, but now years later, all she had to remember her mother by was a single letter, and a lifetime of regret. Elsa was kind in some ways, but she was jealous of Betty, and Betty never did much right in her eyes.

The people from the surrounding farms started to arrive, old and young, in the middle of the big barn the table was set as always. Food in excess was spread across the table, along with lanterns casting a dim glow over everything.

"Have you seen how handsome Uri is?" Betty whispered under her breath.

Amity giggled and shifted in her chair, "I know right? I can still feel his hands on my hips as he helped me on to the horse."

"Oh and weren't they the biggest stronger hands ever?" Betty swooned.

"I'm going to make a play for him you know?" Amity murmured under her breath.

"No you're not, I am, and I've already spent some quality time with him."

Betty wagged her brows and reached for bunch of grapes.

"You can't eat now, we have to say thanks first," Amity said slapping Betty's hand.

"Oh please, no one is even looking."

Betty listened to her friends as they cooed over the newcomer and she opted not to show any interest. They had reason to try and win his affection, she had none. She will see this night through and make the best of a bad situation. Besides, she had a lot more on her mind. Maybe it was time she accepted the fact that she was a spinster, and she figured it was time she spoke to the Bishop and go his take on her moving out of her paternal home into her own. She could always offer her help as a teacher. She knew how to read, in fact she loved reading. She could go spend time at the local school and read to the youngsters, even help the school teachers to give extra lessons in literacy.

"Rachel!" Amity's voice broke into her thoughts.

"Oh... sorry I wasn't listening," she apologised.

"I was saying, maybe all three of us should play for Uri, we can see which one he picks."

Rachel raised her brows, "He's not up for auction, it's a silly game you're wanting to play."

"Stop being such a drab! It will be fun."

No it won't, she thought. The first thing that is bound to happen is that Uri will pick either Betty or Amity, then that will leave one or the other angry and disappointed, ruining a friendship of many years.

"I'm not a drab, I'm just saying. What if he picks Betty, then you'll be angry, not?"

Amity rolled her eyes, "You take things way to seriously, if he picks Betty, then so be it, I'm hardly desperate to marry."

"Come on Rachel, it will be fun; besides, maybe he shows no interest in any of us, then at least we know we all tried."

Betty worried her lip and looked down at her hands, "I don't know, I suppose no harm can come of it." She for one knew that she won't be the least bit phased if he picked Amity or Betty, because she knew she stood no chance.

Amity shoved her elbow into Rachel's ribs and gestured with her head towards the door. Talk of the devil, Uri was heading straight down the path on the opposite side of the table with his eyes fixed on them. And once again the sight of him made her heart race and as she watched him approach it was as if all else around her faded. She had tunnel vision and it was only him looking straight at her. When he finally stopped and took a seat directly opposite her she averted her eyes immediately. Of course, Amity kicked her under the table and Rachel cleared her throat uncomfortably.

"*Hallo* Uri," she said.

"*Hoe gaan het*, Rachel?" he smiled.

She only nodded, her tongue felt like led in her mouth, and her palms were sweaty.

Betty and Amity both fell right into conversation, putting their best foot forward while Rachel wanted nothing but to flee. Soon enough the evening got on the way, with youngsters all frolicking and enjoying the event. Uri made sure he mingled with everyone and never let on that he was interested in any of them in particular, which was funny, since Betty put her best foot forward and out rightly told him he had beautiful eyes.

As the evening drew to a close and most of the people had left, the last remaining few spent the rest of the time talking about the up and coming barn raising event. Uri was still seated across from Rachel, and Betty and Amity had moved closer to where Bishop Gunther was. He was playing the harmonica, which was probably the only instrument allowed in the community, but still sounded like heaven.

"So Rachel, have you always lived here?" Uri asked curiously as he picked on some of the bread sticks on his plate.

"*Jah*, I was born here," she said and offered him a shy smile.

"I'm surprised I don't remember you?"

"I'm not exactly the most memorable of all," she laughed.

"Oh but you are, you are a very beautiful woman."

Rachel blushed profusely and covered the side of her face with her hand, "Thank you," she mumbled.

"Can I pick you up for church on Sunday?"

Shocked at his request, Rachel shifted uncomfortably in her seat and worried her lip, as tempting as it was, she wasn't so sure if it was a good idea. But then again, Betty and Amity did say that they should all try and win his affection. She looked down at her empty plate and smiled. Perhaps it was time she stepped out of her comfort zone and tried dating at least, after all, he was simply going to take her to church, and it wasn't like he was proposing to her at all.

"Sure," she said and then got up, "I have to go now. I will see you around."

She saw his mouth open and close, but she rushed away regardless. She said her goodbyes to her friends and the rest of the community who were all still in the barn and headed home. Her mind was racing and her heart even more. For the life of her she couldn't understand what Uri saw in her. *You're a beautiful woman* – he had said, and it made her feel as if she was about to fly into the night sky on wings of angels. No boy, or man for that matter, had ever paid her such a compliment, and coming from someone as handsome and Uri, made her tummy do strange things.

Chapter 4

Uri was up and ready long before dawn on Sunday, making sure his buggy was clean and that he too was dressed in his best church clothes. He couldn't deny the fact that he felt bad for Betty, she had shown her affection so openly, but there was just no chemistry between them. Unlike Rachel, Betty was just too flamboyant to his liking. She was a pretty woman, but not even nearly as pretty as Rachel. Rachel was unusually pretty, with red hair that always seemed so perfectly plated and rolled up under her prayer cap, with loose strands that tickled her cheeks. The slight dusting of freckles across her nose, that spread to her cheeks made her even prettier, almost innocent not to mention the way she blushed every time he spoke to her.

He was quite surprised when she accepted his request to start off with, but pleased nonetheless.

The first night he saw the shy girl, with her baskets filled with eggs, he was intrigued. She was in control despite the stormy weather and their predicament, and even when he lifted the other two on to the horse, she never uttered as single complaint. She walked quietly next to them as if she was taking a stroll. Not even the rain slanting heavily against them broke through her composure. Maybe it was the way she kept to herself, or the way her eyes lit up the next day when he bumped into her, he wasn't quite sure himself, but if he had to pin it to one thing, it was God's will. It was God's will that he returned to Derby Creek after all these years and God had sent the storm so that he could meet his future wife.

"Uri, you're up early," Betty said as she entered the kitchen where he was having his morning tea.

"Jah, up and ready for church," he said and grinned excitedly.

She came to sit next to him and perched her chin on her hand, looking at him all dreamy eyed. Shifting slightly to get some distance, he smiled and shoved the plate of rusks closer to her.

"I'm on my way to collect Rachel for church," he announced, not sure how Betty would react.

From day one, she had made it no secret that she fancied him; neither did Amity, so it was better if he got it out in the open before either of them got their hopes up.

"Rachel?" Betty said scrunching up her face, "Have you asked her then?"

He nodded and took the last sip of his tea, "Jah, she's a shy one, but she accepted my offer."

Betty scratched her head and slumped back in her chair, and Uri could just imagine what thoughts were flitting through her mind, hoping that this would not ruin their friendship. But when Betty stood up and held her hand up for a high-five, he grinned.

"She's a dear friend, but a nervous wreck, you best make sure you treat her right," Betty grinned, "She's had a lot of hardship with that stepmother of hers."

Uri frowned, tempted to ask about this stepmother, but held back. If anyone was going to tell him about Rachel, it was Rachel herself. He would want for no secrets or tall tales to come from anyone other than her.

He looked at the clock against the wall in the kitchen and took his hat, nodded at Betty and headed out. For a man nearing his thirties, he felt like teenager himself.

~*~

Rachel waited outside for Uri's arrival and her stomach was doing wild flips, while her heart was missing beats every so often trying to keep up the pace. She had never entertained the advances of a man, and had no idea how to behave in the presence of one who had made his intensions clear. A boy simply did not offer a girl a ride in his buggy unless he was interested in her as more than a friend. This was serious business. She also omitted to let her father know, because she knew that Elsa would have a hundred and one things to say about it. She shifted on the swing chair changing her position, trying to find the one that made her feel most at ease, but her body felt awkward. Her arms felt as if they were too long, her legs felt numb and overall her body and mind appeared to be disconnected. Tired of trying to figure out the best seating position she stood up and paced up and down the porch, and then finally she opted for leaning against the pillar. Just in time too, as she heard the nearing rumble of a buggy, which could only have been Uri.

When he came to a stop in front of her gate, she quickly rushed down the stairs.

"Morning Rachel, you look lovely today," Uri said as he climbed out and came around to help her in.

"Good morning," she said softly.

"Did you sleep well?"

"Jah, I did, thank you."

It took her some time to loosen up and say more than four words at a time, but Uri had this amazing ability to make her feel free. With him she didn't have to count every word, or watch her tongue. She could just say what she wanted. On their way to church, he asked her about the things she likes most. The talked about her life, and her family, she didn't feel like she needed to hide anything from him at all. She even admitted how she felt about Elsa, which made her feel less restricted. At church, they didn't sit next to each other, but Betty and Amity were curious as ever.

"So he picked you did he?" Amity whispered under her breath.

"I don't know, maybe," Rachel murmured.

"You're blind as a bat; everyone can see he likes you."

Rachel blushed and kept her head down, her friends were impossible and as much as she tried to pay attention to the service she couldn't. If it wasn't for Betty or Amity, whispering to her under their breaths, it was the sure awareness of Uri watching her. And that did not go unnoticed by her friends either.

By the time the service had come to an end, Rachel couldn't wait to get outside to catch a breath of fresh air, and steal a moment for herself, but it was short lived.

"You never told us you're meeting a boy?" Elsa said as she came to stand next to Rachel.

"I didn't know I needed your permission," Rachel said blankly.

"Well I suppose you are old enough to make your own, but you know, Albert will be very disappointed that you never told him."

Rachel knew exactly what Elsa was playing at, and this time she was not going to let the woman who pretends to care throw any hurdles in her way.

"I think he'll live, and you should be too pleased that I won't be a bother to you for much longer."

Talk about rushing into things, Rachel thought as she hurried away from Elsa, it wasn't as if Uri was going to ask for her hand in marriage, they hardly knew each other. But even if that wasn't the case, whatever happened, come the beginning of winter, she would move out anyway and start her own life, with or without a husband.

Chapter 5

Uri had spent most of the time getting to know Rachel, and the more he got to know her, the more he was convinced that she was the perfect wife for him. He had spent almost every evening visiting with Rachel and in the past few months since they started their courtship he got to know a woman, who despite her adversities in life, rose above it all. Her stepmother no longer tried to boss her around, and her father was too pleased that his only daughter is finally blooming.

It was a perfect autumn day; the ground was covered in a carpet of reds and golds that reminded him of Rachel. He had already asked her father for her hand in marriage, and although it didn't quite follow the custom of dating for an extended period, he saw no reason to wait. They were both adults who were in love and certain of one thing, their own happiness.

As usual he waited patiently for Rachel to exit the house, and like two curious toddlers Amity and Betty was not far away either. They had both come to terms with the fact that he had made his choice, and they were extra supportive of Rachel too. As he whispered a silent prayer for guidance, Rachel made her appearance as if the Lord had answered his prayer. Today was the day he was going to ask her for her hand in person.

"Good morning Uri," she said and her smile lit up his world.

"Morning to you Rachel, you look absolutely radiant today," he complemented her and it earned him an even wider smile.

"I made myself a new dress, do you like it?"

"It's beautiful," he said and held out his hand.

He could already imagine the gasps and giggles coming from the two friends as he struggled to find the right words. He had rehearsed it so well, but now here in the moment, he was at a loss for words.

"Are you alright?" she asked and placed the back of her hand against his cheek, "You look flustered."

Uri cleared his throat and caught her hand, keeping it against his cheek, "I'm fine, but there is something I would like to ask you."

Rachel tilted her head and her hazel eyes sparkled with curiosity as she waited for him to speak.

"Go on!" Betty shouted from across the road!

Uri closed his eyes and smiled, they weren't helping him at all.

"Uri?" Rachel said softly, "What is it?"

He took a deep breath, and then took both her hands in his, "Rachel, I have spoken to your father, and I would be honoured if you would agree to become my wife."

The way Rachel's expression changed from being concerned to completely surprise was priceless. She didn't have to answer him at all, because the way her lips tugged into a wide smile and her eyes filled with tears, he knew she wouldn't turn him down.

Rachel flung her arms around his neck and buried her face in the crook of his neck and whispered, "I thought you'd never ask."

Uri chuckled, "I was hoping you would accept."

"Why would I not?" she said and smiled lovingly up at him.

JOANNA

1.

Tracing her finger over the cold, gray tombstone, Joanna inhaled deeply and choked back a sob. Kneeling in the pasture of their family's cemetery, she placed a bouquet of daffodils in front of the stone. It all felt like a dream to her. She didn't think she would ever lose her mother. She was her best friend and now that she was gone Joanna felt lost. She spoke softly to the stone just as she would as if her mother were standing beside her. "Hello, Mother. I miss you more each day. I really wish you could have stayed. It's lonely here without you. Everyone is trying to be strong. They want to continue life as it was before, but without you being here, it's impossible. I know you're in a better place and you're not in pain from the illness ravaging your earthly body, but it's still hard. I just don't know what to do now. I have assumed all of your household duties, just as you would have wished, but I find myself feeling increasingly empty. None of this feels right." Before she could finish her conversation, she heard the distinctive sound of horses clopping in the distance. She knew her brothers would be coming to take her back to their small home in the center of their community. They would have finished their errands in town, and she would be needed soon to start preparing supper. Dusk would be upon them soon, and after evening services, a good meal, a nice fire, and sleep would be arriving soon.

Joanna stood up slowly and ran her fingers along the cold stone one more time, giving a weak smile of recognition to her brother, Eli, who trotted up on his prized horse, Petunia. Petunia was a gentle creature and was easily broken. Eli was good to the creature and she respected him as well, she wouldn't ever buck him off, even when they were traveling through thunderstorms or if she ran up on a snake in the tall weeds. They trusted one another. Joanna could say the same about her brother, even though she was the older sibling, they trusted one another and vowed to always protect one another through all of life's trials. Eli looked down from Petunia and frowned. He hated to see his sister suffer so, but as a young man, he knew that for the good of the community he couldn't let his own sorrows show. He had to be strong for his sister now and show nothing but unconditional support. Now was the time for them to come together as a family and keep each other close. That's what his mother would have wanted. "It's good to see you, sister. Are you ready to return to the house?"

Joanna looked up at Eli's eyes and knew that behind the deep brown spheres, there was a touch of sadness that lingered there. He was trying so hard to put on a brave front, but she knew the truth, he wouldn't be the same after their mother's passing either. "Yes. I'm ready to return, Eli. Can I ride with you?"

"Of course. I think Petunia has it in her to walk us both back home along the path." The horse merely whinnied and they both laughed at her response. As they trotted along the path, Joanna's voice turned solemn once again as she asked, "How's father today?"

"He didn't say much at all, he merely got up and went into his study, where he read some scriptures and made some notes for service, then he walked out into the garden and surveyed the crops. It was like a typical day for him it seems."

"I wish he would express himself more."

"Ah, you know how he is Joanna, that's how he always was, stoic and stone-faced."

"Yeah. Maybe one day we'll figure him out."

"Ha! You have jokes, my sister. I seriously have my doubts about that."

They rode back up to the house in relative silence only listening to the sounds of the birds chirping and the echo of Petunia's hooves against the ground. Reaching the house, the pair dismounted and Eli walked Petunia to the barn, taking care to make sure she had plenty of fresh hay and water. Joanna went straight into the house and immediately made her way to the kitchen. In her mind's eye, she could still see her mother standing by the stove, stirring a pot or leaning over to get a knife from the bottom drawer. It was up to her now to make sure the family was fed. She sighed heavily and reached up above the family's ice box to take down a larger pot which hung above it. It was cast iron and the same one that had been used in the family for generations to make hearty stews and soups. That night Joanna decided she would make the family a hearty beef stew. They had some extra meat frozen already in the icebox and she had plenty of canned vegetables from the summer and fall's gardening. She poured some water that had already been carried inside into the large cast iron pot and lit the fire beneath their wood and coal stove. When it came to a full boil she added the meat and vegetables. Her mother had always tried to make her stews last for a few days and made it a point to ensure it was filling as well. Joanna added some corn starch to thicken the broth and proceeded to flavor it with spices. When her father walked into the kitchen, he hung his head, but then looked up and met Joanna's eyes, giving her a slight nod of approval. When the preparations were finished Joanna carried the pot along with some freshly baked bread out to the dining room. The family took their assigned places around the square table. In their mourning period, it was customary to set an extra place at the table for the lost as well, so her mother's chair while empty next to her father, had a place setting and was served some stew as well. It would be her father's task to consume it.

2.

After all was seated, her father spoke. "Good evening my son and daughter. Let us all rejoice and give thanks for what the day hath brought forth. Now is the time we must graciously give thanks for the abundance the Lord hath provided us with and draw close together as a family in our hour of need. I was reading the scriptures this morning and they brought me much comfort. Despite our loss, I trust each of my children to go on living and continue to be upstanding and show true grace. Now let us break bread and honor the fallen."

They all opened their eyes and lifted their heads watching their father who broke the first bit of bread. He then passed the plate to the others who took their portions and set the tray back in the center of the table. Their meal was eaten in silence and no one dared to speak until their simple supper was finished. Their father then looked at each of them and smiled. Tufts of white hair showed his age and he had a natural ruddiness to his skin tone that made him look jovial. He also had lines etched along his forehead left by the many years of being contemplative. One would look at him and assume he was a stern man all of the time, but he had crows feet and smile lines along his eyelids that told another story. While their father was stern and quiet, Joanna could remember a time when they were children he would play their games with them and tell stories which made all of them laugh joyously. He was a man dedicated to worship, but he also was a man who prided himself on the family he had created.

Rising from the table Joanna began to gather the dishes and place them in the kitchen sink, as she crossed into the other room she heard her father say, "Joanna, I'm very pleased with all the progress you have made in the kitchen with meal preparations. Your mother, rest her soul, would be very proud of you." Tears formed in Joanna's eyes and she bit her bottom lip to choke back a sob. Her mother, Annabelle, had been gone now for over a month, but the loss still stung. Her entire family was stuck living with the reminders of her being. Joanna still hadn't had the heart to clean out her closet or her sewing room. The elders had planned a town gathering at the end of the month, however, so she thought she would take them then and donate them. After all, she was a practical woman, just like her mother before her, and knew that there was no sense in good pieces of clothing going to waste when someone less fortunate could be using them. She responded to her father when returning to the table for a second trip for the remainder of the dishes.

"Thank you father, I appreciate it. I discover more techniques every day. I feel personal growth is important, don't you?"

"Why, of course it is, Joanna. I've watched you and Eli grow through the years and I'm proud of both of you. I personally feel comforted by the fact that no matter how many times I go to complete a task and fail, I always have another opportunity to give it another try. That's the beauty in salvation and forgiveness. As humans, we all fall short of perfection, but there's always the chance to redeem yourself through prayer and multiple attempts."

Eli cleared his throat and spoke for the first time since they arrived home. "I'm glad for that. I know that there have been many times I felt lost or like I was on the wrong path, but I would pray about it and then something would happen or suddenly change in my life." Joanna listened to the pair talk from the kitchen while washing up the supper dishes and smiled. She loved her father and brother dearly but felt lost. She had no one to talk about her daily affairs with now that her mother had passed. She couldn't tell her father about the gossip she overheard while getting notions for sewing. She couldn't talk to her brother about a certain feeling she had in the pit of her stomach when she watched the baker's son splitting wood while hanging their linens out to dry.

She listened as their conversation continued. Her father spoke in a good-natured tone and there was nothing condescending in his voice as he elaborated on the subject matter with his son. "Eli, do you remember that time you came home crying when you were thirteen or fourteen? It was late in the evening and mid-summer. You had just returned from Mrs. Hollister's barn dance, she was having to raise money for the local town orphanage. You came to me and had tears in your eyes and your lips were swollen and shaking. I'll never forget how dejected you looked."

"Yes, father. I remember that well. I had gone to the dance and got quite upset when I saw Pamela Davison dancing with my friend, James."

"Do you remember what I told you?"

"No, I can't say I can recall, though it must have worked, I haven't harbored feelings for Pamela since that night."

"What I told you then son, was that sometimes we think we know what's best for ourselves, but in the end, it's not us who is ultimately in control of that. Our actions may influence our day to day activities, but it is only through faith we can fulfill our ultimate destiny. Our almighty father wants us to be happy, but sometimes we have to learn a lesson the hard way so we don't pursue other things. Your courtship with Pamela, for example, is one of those things. Do you know what she's doing now?"

"No, father. I haven't a clue."

"She decided to go live among the outsiders. Her life has not been beneficial from it, given my understanding. The last news we received in a letter that she decided to pursue her career as a professional dancer. It turns out that career path led her to work in a nightclub for exotic dancing and she's developed a drug addiction. It's in my best estimation that she will more than likely spend a great deal of her life in prison for drug related crimes or prostitution. So, son, as you can see sometimes our Father doesn't answer our prayers for a reason."

"What if I could have changed her? If she stayed with me, then maybe she would have just lived her life pursuing the path of righteousness."

"Well, I know how susceptible young men are to the wiles of women and their charms. I think that given the choice, you would have left and gone with her and been corrupted by the outside world as well. Outside of our community, there is a temptation to pursue wrongdoing on every corner. No matter what your vice, there is some way to purchase it or attain it there. Never forget that on your travels, Eli."

"I won't Father."

3.

Joanna listened to their conversation while she continued to tidy up the dinner dishes. She knew that her mother would have loved that their father was attempting to socialize with his children, but she also knew that her mother would have played devil advocate in the conversation. She wasn't like most of the other women in the town. She was outspoken and often had heated debates on matters of faith or business with her father, yet they worked to balance each other out very well. Joanna was convinced that when God made her mother, his creation was done purely to spite her father and keep him in line.

She cleaned up the sink and then decided she would go ahead and get the percolator ready for the morning's coffee. She knew that would be the first thing their father would ask for when he woke up in the morning. He often preferred the strong brew first thing, then would go out to complete his chores, foregoing breakfast until their animals had been fed. He always said that if one took care of the animals, they would, in turn, take care of you. He lived by this strict routine day in and day out, with little variation in routine, save for the day he celebrated his wedding anniversary with his wife. On that day, both their father and mother would take a rare trip to town, where they would return with not only small gifts for the children but some goods, that were less costly to purchase such as new blades for the farming equipment. Joanna always dreamed of the outside world as being some type of magical realm where everyone had access to things like running water and life was easy, but as she grew older she realized the outsiders weren't much different than those in her own community. She wasn't allowed to do much traveling into town, but when she did she just noticed that the outsiders seemed to base their own value on their material belongings. This concept just simply didn't exist in her community, everything was shared.

Joanna saw that it was dark now outside and with her chores attended to, she didn't see the point in staying with the menfolk talking around the dinner table. Drying her hands on a dish towel, she decided to go ahead and excuse herself. Walking around the side of the table she approached her father and placed her hand on the side of his chair then leaned over kissing him on the forehead. "I'm going to go ahead and turn in for the evening, father. The nightly chores are all completed."

"Ah, yes, very good little one. My precious daughter. You have sweet dreams and remember that your father and brother are here if you have night terrors."

"Oh, papa. I love you. I haven't had a night terror, though, since I was seven years old."

"Still.. think good thoughts."

"I will. Goodnight. Goodnight Eli."

"Goodnight, sister, remember I love you even in your slumber."

"I will."

Joanna walked to her bedroom and lit the small candle that was on her nightstand, it provided enough light to read by, which is the only thing she enjoyed doing in the evenings to relax. Taking off her bonnet, she sat on the edge of the bed and began undoing the long braids she had in her hair. She preferred to keep it pulled up and away from her face during the course of the day since she was often doing chores. The tresses undid themselves easily and she fluffed hands through it, taking her hairbrush and running it through her long brown locks. After she put on her nightgown and hung her daytime dress back up in her standing closet, she picked up her Bible, seeing the notes she had made in the margins. She had been studying a chapter in Revelations that her father recommended. He felt that it would benefit the family to examine the reasons for death together, so they could make some sense of their mother's unexpected passing. She sighed and remembering her place decided she would finish reading and analyzing the chapter when she arose the following morning. Instead, she picked up the paperback she had borrowed from the town's library. It had a handsome cowboy on the front of it and he appeared in front of a herd of galloping horses. He was holding a blonde woman in his arms and she was swooning. Joanna smiled as the opened the book to the place she left off. It wasn't customary for women in her community to read much at all, but she enjoyed the thoughts of romance and found nothing wrong with dreaming about a handsome cowboy of her own. She finished the chapter and blew out her candle, reclining on her twin bed and closing her eyes sleeping almost immediately.

4.

As the dawn peeked through the clouds, Joanna was awakened by Eli, barging into her bedroom unannounced. He let the door bang on the hinges and had a panicked look on his face, as Joanna pulled the covers up over herself asked, "Why, Eli?! Whatever is the matter?! Is it Father?! Is he okay?!"

"Yes. Oh, Joanna, I'm worried. It's Petunia. She's fallen ill I'm afraid. Can you come out to the barn?"

Breathing out a sigh of relief, Joanna nodded and said, "Of course dear brother. Don't be fearful. The Lord will protect Petunia. Give me a few moments to get decent and I will be out there." Joanna calmly got up from her bed and walked to her closet, taking a few moments to pull her hair back and put on her bonnet then putting on her daytime dress. She pulled the laces tight on her boots and hurried out to the barn where she could see Eli standing by Petunia's stall pacing anxiously. "Thank you for coming out sister. I can't figure out what's wrong with her. She won't respond to my coaxing and she's just lethargic. I've never seen her in this state."

"Calm yourself, Eli. Your panicked state is doing her no good either. Animals can sense your fear." Joanna walked up to the mare who was laying down and looked into Petunia's deep brown eyes. She then placed her hand gently on the creature's forehead. She then stroked the animal's head and back, making soothing sounds, just as her mother would do them when they were sick youngsters. "Yes. You're right to have come to fetch me. She's definitely fallen ill. Let's just hope its a bug. Father has a trip planned to go into town to gather some new ax blades for the fall cutting. I'll go with him and stop by the library and see if I can find a cure in some of the veterinary medicine books they have shelved. Don't worry, brother. We will do what we can for her. Just be fervent in your prayers and there will be a way delivered."

Joanna walked back into the home and began preparing her father's morning coffee. Daylight had just broke and she knew he would be happy to get the day started like normal. When he walked in the kitchen he smiled seeing her standing at the stove as her mother would have, fixing his coffee and preparing breakfast for her brother. Eli always had a voracious appetite She set the steaming mug in front of him and said, "Good morning, Father. I must confess it's already been eventful."

"Oh, really how so?"

"It seems Petunia has fallen ill. I was hoping it would be okay if I went with you while you were in town today to look up some medicine for her at the library."

"I certainly hate to hear that Petunia has taken a turn for the worse. She has been good to our little family. I think that's a wonderful idea darling. God can work miracle cures, but only if we're willing to do a bit of the work as well. After the morning feeding, we will go into town. Be prepared. While I'm purchasing the new blades for the fall wood harvest, you can look into a cure for our Petunia. I bet your brother is worried sick."

"Oh, he is Father. You know he's always been close to the mare."

"We shall do what we can. Thank you for the finely brewed cup of coffee. Now I must get to work, the daylight is already streaming upon us and the chickens will be happy to receive their breakfast."

"Thank you, Father."

Joanna finished making the biscuits and gravy for breakfast then poured them all glasses of freshly squeezed orange juice from the assortment of oranges that they had traded for in town earlier in the summer. She knew their shelf life would be expiring soon and didn't want anything to go to waste. Waste not, want not, her mother always said. She also knew that they all need to keep their strength up because as soon as they got back from town the entire community would gather and chop wood for their collective heat in the winter. After completing her chores and cleaning up the cooking utensils she set the meal on the dining room table and gathered her bag for their trip into town. She made certain she had her city library card and decided to take her paperback with her and exchange it for another as it was nearing completion anyway. Looking around the empty room she sighed. She was worried about her brother, but also she felt a doubt creeping into her soul and a generalized discomfort, wondering if this is how the remainder of her days would be spent, taking care of her father and brother , never knowing the love of a man or having her own family to raise.

Her father and brother came back into the house after feeding the animals and sat down at the table, nodding in appreciation at having their meal already set before them. Eli spoke then, asking to say the morning prayers and included a blessing for his favorite mare as well. They ate the rest of their meal in silence and Joanna immediately went to the sink and began cleaning up the dishes, so she wouldn't have to do both the breakfast and dinner dishes before bed. She also was anticipating having a busy day tending to Petunia upon their return. Her father came and got her when the horses were hitched up to the wagon and her brother helped her climb in beside him. Her father gave his horses a quick pat on the head and they departed on their journey into town.

    5.

Arriving in the nearest town, Joanna took in her surroundings as her father hitched up the wagon to the hitching post by the hardware store. She got out of the buggy, amidst the stares of the townspeople. She imagined she looked quite strange to then in her pale blue day dress, with her hair pinned up in a bonnet, while her father was dressed head to toe in all black, complete with his wide-rimmed black hat. His long brown beard wasn't shaved, merely groomed and it did betray his age, as spots of gray could be seen in it when the sun hit it just right. He spoke briefly to his daughter before going inside the store. "Remember daughter, be polite to the townspeople, but do not engage in lengthy conversation unless it pertains to spreading the Gospel. I will be here when you are ready to leave but try to find the information you seek quickly. I suspect this lost time will hurt our productivity later and we won't be able to get as much done as we should. Be careful, Joanna."

Joanna nodded and hugged her father before crossing the street and rounding the block heading to the library. She cast her eyes downward mostly only looking up periodically to dodge obstacles. She opened the doors to the city library and the pleasant librarian smiled and waved at her when she entered. She smiled back and returned the greeting. She liked the librarian, who never questioned her when she came in even as a little girl clutching her mother's skirts. The older clerk would give her lollipops when her mother checked out her religious books and romance novels. Now Joanna was grown and even though she didn't get a lollipop, she still felt those warm feelings when she was in the library. She walked up to the desk and quietly dropped her book on the counter. "I need to return this, and I will be getting another one if I can find the other information I need in time."

"Sure thing, Joanna. Have you been doing okay, since your mother's passing?"

"Oh, yes we have been doing alright, thank you. I'm sorry I was in such a bad state when you saw me last. I am adjusting to this new normal."

"Well, that's good. If you need anything, you let me know as always."

"I will. I will see you when I return."

Joanna then walked off, smiling once more at the clerk. She rounded the corner to the reference desk where there was no clerk, but there was a younger looking man in grease-stained coveralls standing by the finance books, looking bewildered. Joanna watched him pull out a book from the shelf as the rest came tumbling down. She couldn't stifle a small giggle as he fumbled trying to catch them all. He turned around hearing her laughter and she was met with a sheepish smile and the most striking blue eyes she'd ever seen. He took her by surprise as she felt her heart beat faster within her chest and suddenly heat rose to her face as she blushed deeply. Before she could say a word he smiled broadly at her and said, "They don't make these shelves the way they used to do they?"

Joanna giggled once again and said, "No. They certainly don't."

"I don't really know much about this place. I needed a book on taxes, I own my own mechanic shop and I'm doing my own this year to save money for the business. Maybe I should have just paid someone."

"Well, what are you looking for? Maybe I can help."

"A book to tell me how to do it."

Joanna paused for a moment surveying the shelves then reached down to the bottom one, accidently brushing the man's hand as she picked up a hefty volume and placed it in his arms. "Here you go. This will guide you through the process."

"Oh wow. Thank you. I appreciate that ma'am. It's nice to meet you, my name's David."

"I'm Joanna. I'm not from around here, as you can tell."

David took a step toward her, closing the distance, and Joanna felt a certain electricity pass through them. She let the heat rise to her cheeks again and once more looked into his blue eyes. He was in good shape and looked strong from his work. He had blonde hair and was clean shaven. He didn't look like any of the men from their community, but he did seem to possess the same kindness behind his eyes and good spirit. He responded by saying, "I wish you were from around here. I'd hire you to do my taxes."

She chuckled at his joke, then suddenly remembered her purpose. "I really hate to cut on conversation short, David, but I have to get some information then return to my community, my brother's horse is sick and needs medical attention I know nothing of."

"Oh, I'm sorry to hear that. Maybe I can help. I grew up on a ranch."

She couldn't believe her ears. She had wanted a cowboy all of her own. Could it be that her prayers had been answered? He seemed so genuine and caring. She explained the problem with Petunia and David gave her the information she needed to attend to the mare. He reassured her it was nothing major that some tender loving care couldn't fix. He then went on to say that his specialty in life was fixing broken things. Joanna considered the gravity of his statement before turning to leave and decided to do something she would need to ask forgiveness for later.

"You have been so helpful David, could I have your address?"

"Only if I can have yours too."

The pair exchanged addresses and Joanna exited the library, turning around to see David staring at her making her exit. She didn't know what had come over her, but she knew in her heart this man was her destiny.

6.

She exited the library to find her father standing red-faced by the door, checking his pocket watch. She hadn't realized how much time had passed talking with David, she only knew that it felt like they had known each other a lifetime. Feeling the need to apologize she spoke to her father, when they crossed to the buggy, "I'm sorry, father. It took me longer to get the information I needed than what I thought."

He didn't say anything, but merely nodded and coaxed the horses out of the lot and towards the path back to their community. Her father finally spoke when they were close to the halfway point between town and their village. "You know why we caution each other when talking with townspeople? It's not because our religion has restrictions on being social and making friends. In fact, we are encouraged to witness to everyone we possibly can. It's because not all people are righteous, Joanna. Not everyone will have your best interest at heart, and the original evil does find its way into the hearts of men. Some of the people you encounter in the outside world, well let's say the majority of them, only are interested in preying on the weak. It's their life's goal, not helping others or doing good."

Joanna turned her eyes downward again as her father patted her on the leg continuing, "Remember, no matter what happens, Joanna, your family will always support you within the community. We, however, could not help you should you decide to live among the outsiders. You would be shunned and on your own, you know it's our way, there's no changing that." Joanna nodded in acknowledgment, silently rubbing the piece of paper in her pocket which had David's address on it. She knew in her heart, that she needed to see the mysterious cowboy mechanic once again, but didn't like the idea of her father's disapproval. He would never allow such a thing, she felt conflicted and sick at heart the entire way home.

Arriving back at the community they were greeted by Eli, whose worried look had only grown more exasperated during their time away. "Greetings, Father. Greetings, Sister. Did you acquire the knowledge you sought?"

"I did brother. Let's go to the barn and see what we can do."

Together they walked to the barn and checked on Petunia. Joanna took care to follow David's precise instructions and administered a careful mixture of salt brine and water to the mare who greedily lapped it up. It had seemed that she had just gotten a bit dehydrated during their previous days' activities and was feeling under the weather. They monitored her condition throughout the day and it did improve as she eventually got up and started wandering back and forth in her stall, anxious for a trot. In addition to that the new blade purchase, expedited the wood cutting process and the community made short work of the wood pile, stockpiling enough wood to last the entire winter in half the time it normally would. They decided as a community to celebrate their recent accomplishment and give thanks to the Lord, with a feast to be held that upcoming Saturday night.

Joanna spent the night quietly in her room after supper and allowed herself to think of David. She knew beyond a shadow of a doubt that she needed him in her life. She believed, despite her father's warnings that there were good and decency in his soul. No one without a good heart, would have freely given her that information she needed to help her animal. Most of the outsiders would have offered their services and charged a pretty penny for such knowledge. Joanna thought of the feast Saturday and sighed. Did she want to be stuck in the community all her life, eventually marrying a man who had little passion for anything in life? It was then Joanna made her decision. She would slip away during the barn dance on Saturday and go see David.

As the community was abuzz with the festivities at the dance on Saturday night, Joanna excused herself to go back to the house, hugging her brother and her father tightly before exiting, saying she felt ill and needed to call it an early night. Unnoticed by anyone else in the community, she then proceeded down the well-worn path and made her way to town. She made her way to the address David had scrawled on a ripped piece of an envelope from his coveralls and knocked on his door.

David opened the door, rubbing his eyes, apparently awakened by her rapping. He was groggy but smiled broadly in recognition. "Joanna, is that you are am I dreaming?"

"No. You're not dreaming, David. I'm really here." She paused a moment, considering her options. She thought for a moment about what advice her mother would give her in this moment. She thought back to when she was a little girl clutching on to her mother's skirt, frightened by some imaginary threat. She would have said, "Ah, my precious little girl, there is nothing to be afraid of but your own imagination. If you don't give your fear power over you, you can achieve anything you want in this lifetime." Joanna hesitated a moment then said to David all while blushing and smiling, "I came to be with you David, and hopefully one day be your wife."

David took Joanna by the hand and led her over his front stoop, making sure she didn't trip over the door sill on the way in. When he shut the door behind her he pulled her into his arms and kissed her deeply. Joanna felt a joy like none other she had felt in her life, spread through her bones and body. He then looked deeply into her eyes and said, "Well. I'm not the smartest man you will ever know, nor will I ever be the ideal of perfection, but I promise you this Joanna. I am a decent man with a good heart, and I promise to make this life the best we can possibly have together. So, yes. I do want you to stay with me. You're all I've thought about since I met you that day at the library, and you're all I want to think about for the rest of my days." The pair then walked hand in hand into David's modest living room where they sit side by side on the sofa, holding each other until they drifted off peacefully.

AN AMISH SEASON OF FRIENDS

ELIZA BAKER

Part One:

Steam rose from the grill as Nancy Elliot misted the grill with the spray bottle. She smoothed the front of her apron as she looked around the big industrial kitchen of The Barn, her cousin's restaurant. In the three months since Nancy had moved to Lancaster County, Pennsylvania in the middle of Amish country to help her cousin, Rebecca, run her restaurant, Nancy found that she loved the cozy feeling of the kitchen on nights like this. As autumn had faded into winter, and the days had grown progressively shorter, the brightness and warmth of the restaurant's kitchen had cocooned Nancy as her heart healed. Rebecca had been her cheerleader and her shoulder to cry on.

At the thought of her cousin, Nancy frowned, and glanced at her phone. It wasn't like Rebecca to be late. There weren't many others working tonight as the whole restaurant had been rented out for a wedding rehearsal dinner, but Rebecca should have been there already. She whispered a silent prayer to God that her cousin was okay.

Just as she whispered, "Amen," the back door opened, and Nancy felt her heart lift in relief. As fast as her spirits had lifted, they fell at the sight of Matthew standing there. "Oh, it's you," Nancy said, unable to keep the irritation out of her voice.

Matthew just smiled at her with that infuriatingly calm way he had about him. "Indeed, it is," he said easily. "I told Rebecca that I would be in early to help with prep work. What needs to be done?" Before Nancy could answer, Matthew was already taking off his coat and black felt hat, exchanging them for an apron. "It's icy out there," he commented. "I could barely get my buggy into the stable."

Another shot of worry went through Nancy's stomach. "Rebecca isn't here yet," she blurted out.

"She's probably delayed because of the weather," Matthew said. He gave her a pointed look. "Why don't you call her?"

Nancy blinked at him. Duh, why hadn't she thought of that? Leave it to the Amish guy to point out the obvious. As she yanked her phone back out of her pocket, she thought about what a myth it was that the Amish didn't know anything about technology. Young people like Matthew, who was still in his rumspringa years, knew plenty about the advances in the Englischer world, as they called it. As far as Nancy could tell Matthew had no intention of leaving his rumspringa, or running around, years any time soon. From what she understood that was his time to test the waters in the modern world, and eventually he'd have to make a decision whether or not he wanted to join the Amish church.

The phone continued to ring, and Nancy's mind drifted to her own church that she had left back home. In a way, she was in her own time of decision, although she had literally run away. If she went back to her hometown, she would need to make the decision about whether or not she wanted to go back to her church and face Lily and Jason, her exes. Ex-best friend and ex-boyfriend.

Rebecca's phone went to voicemail, and Nancy felt her stomach tighten into a knot. "Hey, cuz," she said, forcing her voice to be light as she continued the voicemail. "Just wondering where you are. Matthew is here, so we'll start the prep work before everyone else gets here. The wedding party is supposed to be here around seven, right?"

"I'm sure she's just delayed because of the weather," Matthew repeated, still in the same calm voice that he always spoke in. "She probably just doesn't want to answer the phone while she's driving."

Nancy shot him a look of annoyance, her default look with him. "What would you know about that? It's not like you've ever been behind the wheel of a car," she snapped, instantly feeling ashamed of herself. Whenever she got near Matthew, she became her most un-Christian self, and she couldn't figure out why, no matter how hard she prayed about it.

Matthew just smiled wider. "Driving a buggy isn't so different than driving a car," he replied. "And I wouldn't use a phone in this weather even if I was walking."

Letting out an exasperated breath, Nancy said, "Fine, maybe you're right. Let's just get the prep done. The wedding party will be here in no time, and since no one else seems to be showing up for work, I guess it'll just be the two of us for now."

She tried not to notice how Matthew hummed to himself as he started putting together the stuffed mushrooms for the appetizers. Rebecca often commented on how cute Matthew was, but even if Nancy could see his good looks objectively, her heart was so guarded that she never agreed with her cousin. Still, for some reason tonight, she was having a hard time keeping herself as aloof as she wanted to be. Better that she focus on her irritation with him instead. She couldn't risk letting her heart connect with another man, even just as a friend. She was here to work, to spend time with her cousin, and to heal. That was it.

"What are you humming?" she asked, unable to keep her curiosity at bay. She kept facing her cutting board where she was chopping potatoes for the gravy fries.

"How Great Thou Art," Matthew replied.

"Really? That's one of my favorite hymns too," Nancy replied, confusion lacing her voice.

"What's wrong?" Matthew asked.

Nancy shrugged. "I guess I didn't know you, I mean, the Amish in general, had the same hymns as other Christians."

Matthew paused. "You know there aren't that many differences between the Amish and other Christians. There are a lot of misconceptions."

Glancing over her shoulder, Nancy considered him. She nodded. "I suppose there is a lot to learn."

Part Two:

An hour later Nancy and Matthew were still the only ones at The Barn. The knot in Nancy's stomach had continued to tighten as she tried to call Rebecca three more times. She tried not to let her imagination run wild, but she couldn't help but worry. The only upside of her nervous energy was that she moved faster through the prep work than normal, and the two of them finished with time to spare.

"It's really coming down out there," Matthew commented, peering out the back door of the kitchen.

Nancy went to join him. "Do you think the wedding party will cancel? I wish I could get ahold of Rebecca."

Frost formed on the window pane from their warm breath. Matthew cleared his throat. "Well, if the wedding party doesn't come, we'll have a lot of leftover food."

"Rebecca won't like that," Nancy said, frowning. Again the thought of her cousin made the knot in her stomach tighten so painfully that she thought she might throw up.

"We'll just have to eat all of it," Matthew said, giving her a sly grin.

The usual irritation she felt with him flared again, but this time she had to admit that it was mainly irritation with herself since she had just had the same thought. Pushing both her palms against the coolness of the window, Nancy sighed. She wasn't sure what was keeping Rebecca, and it was taking all her might to push the dark, scary thoughts from her mind. No matter what, her cousin would want her to carry on with the operation of the restaurant.

"We should get back to work," Nancy said with a sigh. Matthew looked over at her, and raised an eyebrow. Nancy was surprised to find that she wanted to stay this way, looking into his eyes. Matthew had such nice blue eyes. She shook herself away from the thought, and repeated, "We should get back to work."

Matthew nodded, and walked back toward the kitchen, humming again. Nancy followed after she allowed herself a moment to catch her breath. She hadn't even realized that she had been holding it. Once she got back into the kitchen, she looked up at the clock hanging above the door. There was only twenty minutes before the wedding party was set to arrive. None of the other servers had arrived, and given how bad it looked outside, Nancy wasn't surprised.

"Do you think that anyone else will be able to get here?" she asked as Matthew put the salmon cakes into the oven.

"Honestly? I don't think anyone else is coming out tonight," he said. "Have you checked the answering machine in the office to see if the wedding party has cancelled?"

Again, Nancy felt her cheeks flamed as she realized that Matthew had pointed out the obvious yet again. "I was just going to do that," she muttered.

Even though she turned away quickly, she wasn't fast enough to miss the smirk on Matthew's face. He found her amusing, but instead of annoying her, she felt pleased. And that wasn't something that she could reconcile easily with the fact that her heart had been smashed into a million pieces a mere three months ago. Surely her heart hadn't healed enough to allow her to feel a spark of interest in another man, least of all Matthew. She couldn't even stand him, could she?

"Lord," she whispered, "just show me the way. Amen."

Her relationship with God had been tenuous these past three months, but she kept trying despite the void that seemed to gape open in her heart. Nancy stopped in the middle of the hallway as she realized that she hadn't felt that void in quite some time. Maybe that did mean that her heart was healing. That was a scary thought.

Slipping into Rebecca's office, she walked over to answering machine, which had always seemed so quaint to her. There was no blinking light. Nancy's heart sank. She didn't care if the wedding party came or not—she and Matthew were ready, and with some hustling they could cover the serving—but she had been hoping that Rebecca would have called. She couldn't have admitted it to Matthew, but she was worried, far more worried than she could let on.

Nancy pulled out her cell phone again, and swiped at her cousin's number with a shaking thumb. "Come on, Rebecca," she muttered. The phone went straight to voicemail, and Nancy felt her throat tighten. For a moment she couldn't breathe.

She hurried back to the kitchen, and burst through the door. Matthew looked up from where he was putting the finishing touches on the homemade pudding cups that the bride had requested for dessert. "Did they cancel?" he asked, and he looked so adorable with the hopeful expression on his face that Nancy felt her spirit lift slightly.

Shaking her head, she said, "No, I guess they're still coming, but Rebecca didn't call either. And I still can't get ahold of her. I'm worried."

Matthew set down the spoon on the counter, and said, "I know you're worried, but I'm sure she's fine. Maybe her phone's battery died."

"Maybe," Nancy agreed. Her mind was whirling as she said another silent prayer for the Lord to keep her cousin safe. Before she could say anything else, the bell chimed that signified that the front door was opened. Both she and Matthew startled. "Oh! That must be the wedding party," she said.

Matthew pulled a mock sad face. "Darn, I was looking forward to eating all this pudding," he said.

Nancy knew that she had no choice but to pull herself together to run the restaurant no matter where Rebecca was at the moment. "Keep one set aside for yourself," she said, forcing herself to smile. "I'll go greet the wedding party."

"I'll come with you," Matthew said. He wiped his hands on his apron, and then took it off. "Don't worry, I'm in this with you."

"Thanks," Nancy said, but silently she thought that that might be part of the problem.

Part Three:

"They seem like they are having fun," Nancy commented, peering out of the kitchen doorway window.

Matthew had built a fire in the big stone fireplace that took up most of one wall, and in Nancy's opinion was one of the most impressive features of The Barn. She had turned on some soft jazz on the PA system. A few of the members of the wedding party were dancing, though the music didn't exactly lend itself well to that activity.

"Should we take the appetizers out now?" Matthew asked.

Nancy glanced at the clock, and wished again that she should get ahold of Rebecca. Her stomach was still twisted into a tight knot, but she was trying her best to take Matthew's advice and focus on the most probable scenarios, like Rebecca's phone being out of charge.

"Yeah, we probably should," Nancy said. "Oh, but we should pray over the food first. That's what Rebecca does when she does a wedding rehearsal."

"Right," Matthew said with a nod. "I can offer the blessing, if you'd like."

"That would be great," Nancy said, letting out a sigh of relief. Ever since Jason and Lily had betrayed her she hadn't been able to utter any words of praise out loud. She had just recently allowed herself to relax enough in prayer that she could say words of thanksgiving. So she was grateful that Matthew was offering to pray.

"Dear Heavenly Father," he began as the two of them bowed their heads with their hands extended over the food. "Bless this food as it goes to nourish our guests. Please let them feel the spirit of hospitality that you admonish us to have in Hebrews 13:2, 'Be not forgetful to entertain strangers: for thereby some have entertained angels unawares.' Amen."

"Amen," Nancy echoed. She had a strange sense of disappointment, and she felt like a fool for even feeling that way in the first place. What had she expected? That the Amish had some secret way to pray? She was glad that she managed to keep her mouth closed, and not embarrass herself further.

Each of them picked up a tray of stuffed mushrooms, and Nancy followed Matthew out of the kitchen. The wedding party clapped appreciatively as Nancy and Matthew began to circulate through the small crowd with the first of the food. For the first time Nancy realized that there were only about twenty people there, while the original dinner had been intended for forty. The weather must have kept the other half of the guests at home. Still, those who had braved the weather looked delighted to be there, and that made pride swell in Nancy's chest, pride in Rebecca, pride in being part of something so memorable. She was truly glad that she was there that night.

After most of the mushrooms had been grabbed, Nancy paused as she made her way back to the kitchen. She gazed out the big two-story, floor to ceiling windows that faced the front of the restaurant. Big, white snowflakes were drifting down to the ground, and just beyond the parking lot lights, Nancy could see that the trees were bending in an apparently wild wind.

"The storm must really be picking up," she commented as Matthew moved past her. He paused to look out the window with her. Something crossed his face, some emotion that she couldn't read, and before she could ask him about it, there was a scream from across the room. Both of them turned in alarm.

"She's choking!" someone yelled.

"No, I think she's allergic!" someone else countered. "She's in anaphylactic shock!"

Nancy felt her breath catch in her throat. She turned to Matthew. "I think there's an Epi-pen in the emergency kit in the kitchen. I'll go get it."

"And I'll see what I can do to help," he said, already putting his tray down on a nearby table.

"Have someone call 911," Nancy reminded him as she sprinted back into the kitchen.

Her heart was threatening to pound out of her chest. She skidded to a stop inside Rebecca's office, her eyes scanning the small room for the big white box with the red cross on it. Hadn't she just seen it earlier today when she was checking for messages on the answering machine? The answering machine! That was it! The first aid kit was next to the answering machine. As Nancy made to grab the kit, she noticed that there was a flashing light on the answering machine and her breath caught. There could be a message from Rebecca.

For an instant, she was torn. Everything in her wanted to check the messages, but she knew that she needed to get out to the dining room with the first aid kit. She could feel God prompting her to move her feet, so she did.

When she burst back into the dining room, she stopped short. The wedding party was laughing, and Matthew was standing in the middle of the group apparently scolding a teenage girl. Nancy edged closer so she could hear what was being said.

"Just because you don't like something doesn't mean you can pretend to choke or go into some allergic fit," he was saying. "You scared your mother half to death, and we nearly called 911. On a night like this emergency personnel need to be free to attend to real emergencies. Next time just tell one of the wait staff, and we can find you something else to eat."

"I'm sorry," the girl said plaintively.

Nancy couldn't decide whether she was amused or annoyed, but the one thought that seemed to be consistent was that she really did have a lot to learn about Matthew.

Part Four:

"These salmon cakes are ah-may-zing," the bride-to-be said. She'd already had three or four glasses of wine so she was passing tipsy. The groom-to-be gave Nancy a mild smile, and raised his own glass of wine as Nancy cleared their plates.

When she came back into the kitchen, she wiped the sweat off her forehead with the back of her wrist. "There's no way you would know there's a blizzard out there," she mumbled.

Matthew gave her a sideways grin. "The party seems to be going well, though," he said.

Nancy nodded. "Exactly like Rebecca would want." As she mentioned her cousin's name, Nancy remembered the blinking light on the answering machine. "I'll be right back," she said.

Matthew just nodded as she hurried from the room. As she went into Rebecca's office, she wondered how she hadn't noticed before how easy going Matthew was or how easy he was to talk to. She pushed the thoughts from her head as she crossed the small space to the answering machine. The light was still blinking.

Taking a deep breath, Nancy pushed the play button on the machine. There was a squeak, and then static. Her heart sank. Maybe it had been Rebecca trying to call her to let her know that she was okay, but maybe it was a call from Rebecca to let her know that something was wrong.

Nancy couldn't help but slump back into the kitchen. "What's wrong?" Matthew asked when he caught sight of her.

With a shrug, Nancy said, "There was a message on the answering machine, or well, someone tried to leave a message, but all I could hear was static. I thought maybe it was Rebecca calling to let me know where she is. I can't help it; I'm worried about her."

Matthew set the dishes he was washing back into the soapy water in the sink, and he dried his hands on a towel sitting on the counter. When he came over to Nancy, he put his hand on her shoulder. As he looked deeply into her eyes, Nancy felt a sense of calm wash over her. "Don't let your imagination run away with you," he advised. "I'm sure that Rebecca is fine. If she wasn't surely someone would have called your cell phone, right?"

Nancy nodded. "You're right." She took a deep breath, suddenly hyper aware of his hand on her shoulder. The two of them stared at each other for a long minute. Nancy was vaguely aware of the distant murmur of voices from the party, but in that moment all she could see was the compassion in Matthew's deep brown eyes. His hair needed to be cut, and it flopped forward into his eyes as he leaned down. For a moment, Nancy thought that he might kiss her, and she was surprised to feel excitement rising in her chest at the prospect.

Then Matthew said, "I think I should run out to the stable and check on my horse." He cleared his throat, and dropped his hand.

Nancy blinked, a dazed feeling rolling over her. "Oh, yeah, of course. Be careful out there. It looks like the snow is really piling up. Or at least, I mean it looked that way when I was out there picking up the dinner plates." Nancy stopped as she realized that she was babbling. She took a deep breath, and smiled, "I better get back out there and find out if they want their dessert. You go check on your horse."

Nancy left the kitchen kicking herself as confusion washed over her. She had been so certain that she wasn't ready to open her heart, but here she was hoping that her coworker would kiss her. Her Amish coworker nonetheless. Did the Amish even kiss before they were engaged? Married? She didn't know, and she certainly couldn't ask Matthew. As if that wouldn't be beyond embarrassing.

The bride had filled another glass of wine for herself, and she was in front of the fireplace, twirling in circles, wine glass extended in her hand above her head. She was singing to the jazz music coming through the speakers. She was making up her own lyrics, and even though she was clearly drunk, she seemed so happy. Nancy found herself feeling jealous of the woman. This shocked her almost as much as her desire to have Matthew kiss her. Something was happening inside of her that she hadn't thought would happen for a very long time. God was answering her prayers, was working in her heart.

Shaking her head to clear her thoughts, she offered a silent prayer of thanksgiving to God, and then offered her heart. She knew she needed to be worked on by the Lord. Feeling a new sense of joy springing up in her heart, Nancy smiled genuinely at the groom-to-be as she approached his table.

"Would you guys like your dessert now or in twenty minutes?" she asked.

"Half an hour would be better," he said. "It's not like any of us are in a rush to leave. My mom just called, and she advised us not to even leave for at least an hour or two. That's all right, isn't it?"

Nancy smiled, and said, "Yeah, of course. Just relax and enjoy yourselves. We'll bring out dessert in half an hour. If you need anything, just come find me in the kitchen."

When she got back to the kitchen, Matthew was sitting on the counter eating one of the cups of pudding. He grinned at her, and said, "It's not like we don't have enough."

"How is your horse?" Nancy asked, trying to suppress the desire to hop up on the counter and grab a pudding right along with him.

"Great actually," he said, taking another bite. "Rebecca made sure the stables are perfect. That's a nice perk for her Amish employees. She's a good boss."

At the mention of her cousin, Nancy felt her spirits dip a little. Pushing her worries aside, she walked toward the counter, and hopped up next to Matthew. Grabbing a pudding cup, she dug in.

And then the lights went out.

Part Five:

A moment later the generator kicked on, and the lights came back up. Nancy could hear the guests in the dining room moving around, but no one seemed alarmed. "I'm going to check on the guests," she said, jumping back down.

"I'll come with you," Matthew said.

The wedding party was lounging on the floor by the fireplace. When the bride-to-be saw Nancy coming, she called, "I love this place! I'm having so much fun here! I wish we could get married here. Hey," she said, turning to her groom-to-be, "can we get married here?"

The groom-to-be turned to Nancy and Matthew. "Could either of you marry us here tonight?"

"No, I don't think so," Nancy said. "But I'm glad you're having a good time. It seems like we might be stuck here for a while."

"I don't care," the bride-to-be called. "I would move in here if I could."

"Do you want to have your dessert yet?" Matthew asked.

"Maybe later," someone called.

"So what do we do now?" Matthew asked as he and Nancy walked back to the kitchen. "It seems like we don't have anything to do at the moment."

"Oh, hey, do you want to see something really cool?" Nancy asked. "Only Rebecca and I know about it."

"Sure," Matthew said. She glanced at him with a smile, thinking again how agreeable he was.

Nancy led him through the kitchen, and into the little janitor's closet that was right next to the back door. Moving aside one of the shelving units, Nancy pointed to the ladder attached to the wall. "Follow me," she said.

"Where does this go? The roof?" Matthew asked. "If it goes outside maybe we should reconsider this, save it for some other time, like next summer?"

Nancy was already halfway up the ladder. She glanced back over her shoulder at him with a smile. "Now who is worrying? It doesn't go outside. Now come on, climb."

She led him up through a trap door in the ceiling. When they were both up the ladder, Nancy flicked a light switch, and soft light flooded the small space. "This is the old hay loft. Rebecca turned it into a little retreat if she needed a break. It's cool, huh?"

Once they were settled into the two recliners that had been up here since the restaurant had been renovated , Nancy pointed to the skylight, where snow was piling up at an alarming rate. "We might not be able to get out of here tonight," she commented. She sat up straight as a horrible thought occurred to her. "What will we do with all the guests down there?"

"You really do worry a lot, don't you?" Matthew said. "You need to just let go, and trust God. He'll take care of everything."

Nancy took a deep breath, and let it go. "I can't help it," she said with a sigh as she sank back into the recliner. "You're right, God will take care of all of this." She was silent for a moment. "It's just that I'm getting back to the part of my relationship with God where I feel comfortable trusting Him again."

Matthew was silent for a long moment. "Do you mind if I ask you why?"

Nancy chewed her lower lip as she considered what to say, finally she said, "It's the reason I came here actually. I guess I was sort of running away. The short story is that my ex-boyfriend dumped me to date my ex-best friend. The pain was just so intense that I had to get away. I was so mad at God. I was, am, a good Christian so why would He let anything bad like that happen to me?" The words poured out of her, and despite her mild embarrassment, she felt relief at having finally told her story to someone. Rebecca was the only person who knew the whole story.

Matthew was silent again for a long stretch. Nancy was beginning to realize that was what he did when he wanted to think of a response. She was afraid that he was judging her, but that didn't seem to be in his character so she told herself to calm down.

"I can't tell you that I understand exactly what you have gone through, but my fiancée left me for my cousin," Matthew said softly.

Nancy looked over at him, and saw familiar pain in his eyes, pain that mirrored her own. "How...how did you get through it? The pain, I mean? Sometimes it hurts so much that I worry it will split me in half."

"Time," he replied, leaning back against the recliner and gazed up at the snow covered skylight.

"Time passes slowly," Nancy said with a sigh.

The two of them fell into silence again. Sharing the deepest hurt of her life had made it seem suddenly easier to bear. She liked having someone to share that with, she had missed that after both Jason and Lily were out of her life.

After a moment, Nancy asked, "Were you ever able to forgive them?"

"I did," Matthew replied. "It took me a long time. And there are still times when I see them at family events that it's still hard for me to see them."

"So...they're married?" Nancy asked. The idea of Lily and Jason getting married horrified her...and yet part of her could see that happening. If she was honest with herself, she could see how well suited they were for each other. She and Jason had never been a good match, and she had known that from the beginning.

"They are," he said. "It was a long time ago, though, so it's okay, but yeah, it can be hard."

As they settled back again, Nancy wondered if this was the beginning of the healing she had been praying for.

Part Six:

"Hey, we need to get back downstairs."

Nancy blinked awake to the sound of Matthew's voice. "What, huh?" she asked.

"You fell asleep," he said. "I let you doze for twenty minutes, but your phone has been buzzing for the past five minutes. I think probably better get down to the guests."

"You're right," Nancy said, sitting up straight and rubbing her eyes. "Thanks for the nap, I guess I really needed it."

Matthew led the way down the ladder, and as soon as they got into the kitchen he grabbed the pudding cups. Nancy started to follow him, but he turned to her and said, "You should check to see who was calling you. It might be Rebecca."

"Thanks," she said, feeling her heart squeeze with emotion.

She watched him go, so many conflicting emotions warring in her chest. She didn't have time to sort through them now. She needed to check her phone. Matthew was right. It could have been Rebecca calling, and that was important. More important than anything else at the moment.

She pulled up her phone, and looked at the call history. Sure enough there were three missed calls from Rebecca. Sighing with relief, Nancy pulled her cousin's number up, and chewed on the inside of her cheek while she waited for Rebecca to pick up.

When her cousin did, Nancy cried, "Where have you been? I've been trying to call you for hours! I've been so worried!"

Rebecca laughed—she actually had the audacity to laugh—and said, "I knew you'd be worrying yourself sick about me, and I'm so sorry about that. I dropped my phone in the snow. I wasn't actually sure it would work again."

Nancy huffed out an annoyed breath, but said, "I'm glad that you're okay."

"Thanks, and again, I'm sorry. So, did the wedding party cancel? Did you do a ton of work that we'll have to trash?" Rebecca asked.

"Actually no, they're here right now," Nancy said. "The wedding party, I mean. We're just serving them dessert."

"We?" Rebecca repeated. "I would have thought that all the staff would have called off tonight. I knew you were there, though, and I've been worrying about you all night, having to do all the work by yourself only to have it thrown away."

"Oh, well, it's just me and Matthew, but we're doing fine," Nancy said. "Oh, and this bride is going to give The Barn an outstanding review. I think she wants to move in here."

"Well, that's good to hear, if not slightly odd, but I'll take it," Rebecca said with a laugh.

"I'm glad that you're okay," Nancy repeated. "I don't know if I've told you how much I appreciate the opportunity you gave me to get away from Jason and Lily so that I could heal."

"I'm glad to do it," Rebecca said. "The Lord leads us in strange ways, but they always lead us somewhere better than we could have gotten on our own."

"That's true," Nancy said.

After the cousins had gotten off the phone, Nancy started to clean up the kitchen. Matthew had been out in the dining room for a long time, and she was just beginning to wonder if she should go out and help him when he walked through the swinging door.

"I gave them that old boom box that was sitting in the corner of the dining room. There were a few CDs too. The bride-to-be wants to have a dance party," Matthew said with a smile.

"Hey, they need to have fun," Nancy said. "This is the night before their wedding, and I have a feeling that we'll be here for quite a while yet."

"Was that Rebecca who was calling you?" Matthew asked.

Nancy nodded. "She's fine. She dropped her phone in the snow. Everything worked out, just like you said it would."

"I'm glad," Matthew said, and Nancy was grateful that he didn't gloat. She remembered the way Jason would smirk when he was right about something. That had only ever increased her anxiety. Slowly, but surely she was beginning to see just how the Lord had been protecting her from a future that wouldn't be good for her.

And the Lord had brought her here, to this moment with Matthew. When she looked up into his big brown eyes, she felt a spark of something that she hadn't felt in a long time. She felt the overwhelming need to share her thoughts with Matthew. Taking a deep breath, she said, "I want you to know how much I've appreciated how...kind you've been tonight. Not just helping me with the food and the guests, but helping me with, well, me."

"I've liked you since you started working here," Matthew admitted. "But you seemed so set on hating me that I didn't dare approach you."

"I told you why my heart was closed," Nancy said, spreading her fingers wide in a helpless gesture.

Matthew took a step closer to her. "I know, and I'm glad you shared that with me. I just wish it could have happened sooner. I feel like we spent three months just wasting time that we could have spent working on our happiness."

Nancy nodded. "Part of me agrees with you, but the other part knows that I needed that time to heal."

"The Lord does good things even in the midst of pain," Matthew said.

"And He moves our lives down pathways that we couldn't see for ourselves," Nancy added.

Matthew took another step closer to her. In the dining room, the wedding party had cranked up some dance music, and outside the wind howled, but in the cozy warmth of the kitchen, Nancy felt like she was cocooned in her own world.

As Matthew leaned down to brush a kiss across her lips, Nancy felt joy burst in her chest in fireworks of happiness. She knew that there were more questions than answers about their future, but she was confident that the Lord had led them together for a reason, and instead of worrying, she decided to trust His plan for her, for them.

The End